S0-ANN-390

LOWLANDS

Terence Gallagher

Livingston Press

The University of West Alabama

Copyright © 2017 Terence Gallagher
All rights reserved, including electronic text

ISBN 13: 978-1-60489-190-4, hardcover
ISBN 13: 978-1-60489-191-1, trade paper
ISBN: 1-60489-190-4, hardcover
ISBN: 1-60489-191-2 trade paper
Library of Congress Control Number 2016962957
Printed on acid-free paper
by Publishers Graphics
Printed in the United States of America
Hardcover binding by: Heckman Bindery
Typesetting and page layout: Amanda Nolin, Joe Taylor,
Teresa Boykin, and Sarah Coffey
Proofreading: Joe Taylor, Ciara Denson, Hannah Evans,
Jessica Gonzalez, Jessie Hagler
Cover design: Amanda Nolin, Callie Murphy

Cover photo: a-ma-seul-desire, tapesty courtesy
Musée National de Moyen Âge (formerly Musée de Cluny)

This is a work of fiction:
any resemblance
to persons living or dead is coincidental.

Livingston Press is part of The University of West Alabama,
and thereby has non-profit status.
Donations are tax-deductible:
brothers and sisters, we need 'em.

first edition
6 5 4 3 3 2 1

LOWLANDS

Terence Gallagher

Parentibus meis

CONTENTS

The love that I have chosen
I'll therewith be content
And the salt sea shall be frozen
Before that I repent
– The Lowlands of Holland (song)

1. The Girl

The day I took up my part in this tale, I was walking home from school late Wednesday afternoon. The school bus always let me off about a mile from my house, and I walked from there, wrestling with my heavy brown book bag the whole way; I never could get the strap to sit right.

It was early March. I know the exact day, because I was keeping a diary at the time, in a manner of speaking. I tried to keep a diary a few times when I was young, but I didn't really have the interest. I only tried at all in imitation of my sister, who kept volumes. Within a few weeks, my entries always dwindled to cryptic notes. Within a few months, even those ceased. By a stroke of luck, however, all this happened during one of my rare active periods. Just a word here and there helps me remember, and helps me keep things in their proper order.

My entry for the day was this:

"Saw fuzzy-haired girl on the way home from school"

I was almost home when I saw her. It had been a good walk, despite the heavy book bag. The last holdouts of pockmarked dirty snow had almost all melted away, and you could smell the earth, even in Queens, as the spring shoots broke through. With the approach of Spring, the icy grip of school began to weaken on our hearts. This was the real living myth of youth: the Ogre was dying again.

I was only a couple of blocks from my house when I saw the fuzzy-haired girl looking at me. She was standing straddling a bicycle on the sidewalk across the street, watching me intently. She had dark hair and freckles, and a long nose. I thought she looked foreign. She had a keen pure expression that didn't look American; we tend to be puffier and more diffuse. The bicycle looked old; so did her clothes.

It embarrassed me to be stared at so unambiguously, so I turned away from her and applied myself to walking. When I looked her way again, she was still staring at me. She narrowed her eyes and nodded faintly. She seemed to have satisfied herself of something. She hopped on her bicycle and rode around the corner without a backward glance.

When I got home, I found my father raking leaves in the back yard. He had been away on a business trip. That was new for him. He worked at the academic division of a mid-size publishing house, and they were trying to expand, capture new markets, move into electronic publishing. So they poked my poor father out from behind his desk, and sent him forth. A man less suited for the role of salesman I have seldom seen. I knew it even then. As soon as he got home, he must have jumped into his old clothes and lost himself in dirt and old leaves. We were the only people on the block who still raked leaves. As far as I knew, we were the only people in the city who raked leaves. Everyone else had crews of Mexicans with gas-powered leaf blowers. My father and I raked and bagged whatever we found the time for in the fall. Then we let the remainder sit for the winter. When the last snow melted in the spring he went out again and cleared the wet old leaves. We had a big oak in the back yard, and its tough leaves lasted the winter quite well. We didn't have much of a lawn.

I liked raking. I loved the smell of the wet spring earth, and the sound of the flexible rake tines, and the look of the furrows they left. I heard my father singing to himself, and I knew the song:

> *Cosher Bailey went to college*
> *for to gain some extra knowledge*
> *Studied barmaids at the station*
> *and forgot matriculation*

Did you ever see, did you ever see, did you ever see
Such a funny thing before?

"Hi, Dad, how was your trip?"

My father made a movement of his head, as if to say "it was a trip."

"Glad to be back. It wasn't bad though, as such things go. The crocuses are up."

Years ago, someone planted crocuses in our yard. It might have been a previous owner, it might have been us. No one could remember. We never touched them, but they gradually spread throughout the yard. Every year we had a regular sequence of bulbs and wildflowers that made their appearance. They were the only plants that did well under the shade of the oak.

When I went inside, my mother was already working on dinner. I got home from school late, usually after 5:30, and we tended to eat fairly early, so she had often started dinner by the time I arrived. She would have been singing, too, though I don't remember the song. We were the only family I knew that sang as a matter of course. None of us had any pretensions, or any voices to speak of, although people always talked about my grandmother's voice and how she used to sing.

I had to wait before going up to my room, because my grandfather was heavily descending our sagging old wooden stairs, one careful step after another.

"Hello, James," he said when he saw me. "Out on liberty? Sorry to make you wait. They're right, 'The legs go first.' I haven't been walking enough. Now that the weather is getting better, I should start walking again."

I never minded waiting for my grandfather. "Maybe we can go down the park on Saturday," I said.

When I got upstairs and out of my school clothes, I laid on my bed and listened to the sounds below me. I used to like listening to my family gather and my mother bang pots. My father came in from the yard, and went with my grandfather to listen to the news on television, where I knew they would maintain a relentlessly skeptical commentary. My sister would play the piano until dinner was almost ready, then she'd come in and set the table. We almost always ate together as a family, which was another thing that set us apart. My sister was a couple of years older than me, so she would go out with her friends sometimes, but she usually ate with us. She had a new set of high school friends, but I don't think she liked them very much, so mostly she stayed home and practiced music or read old novels.

So I laid, and I listened, and looked out the window at the birds flying and settling among the empty branches.

2.

My grandfather and I drove down to the park for our walk Saturday morning. It was little more than a mile from our house. We made a long slow circuit along the main path, around a wide field, muddy from the melted snow and the early spring rains. There were a few little ball fields next to the path, but it was still too early for the Little Leaguers to be out practicing. It was an overcast day, and the only other people in the park were dog walkers. I remember a big Great Dane galloping through the mud and slinging its head around as it turned to run back to its master. My grandfather told me it was a harlequin. Once it passed close, breathing heavily, but it paid us no mind. Its master was sitting on a park bench talking into a cell phone. We could hear him clear across the field. My grandfather had a horror of cell phones, and regarded each new technological advance as a fresh calamity. "They have **pictures** now?" He would say in dismay. "They can get the Internet through their **phones**?" My sister and I kept him informed of the latest outrages.

His legs felt strong, so we left the park for our customary detour. My grandmother's old home was just a few blocks from the park. It was the house she had left to marry my grandfather. He liked to come by and visit it from time to time, although anyone connected to them had passed on long ago. He would stand on the sidewalk and point things out with his black walking stick, and tell me things he had told me before. This time, though, he stood in silence, for the house was gone. Builders had come in the winter and torn the house down, and we were left looking at the damp plywood fence protecting the construction site, and at a series of construction permits under plastic, tacked to the wood. My grandfather peered at the permits for a while without reading them. Then we both looked through the gap in the fence where the gate was padlocked shut. They hadn't yet begun on the new foundations. It was all mud; we were standing in it.

"Isn't that something?" said my grandfather. "Isn't that something? They took it down. There was nothing wrong with that house. It was still a good house."

"They're probably putting up another McMansion," I said.

"It was a good house," he repeated. "I'm glad I didn't see them tear it down."

He looked up the street for a moment, and then back at the house.

"Well, that's another one gone. Let's go back to the car."

When we were sitting in the car again, he asked me, "Are you in a hurry? Do you mind if we take a drive?"

So we drove through the neighborhoods, and visited the places that my grandfather remembered. Our family had lived in the area for a few generations, and there were landmarks scattered all about: schools, homes, stores, a parish hall where dances were held. It was not a happy drive, for my grandfather mostly showed me sites where buildings had once stood. Bakeries were gone, German butcher shops, Italian fish stores. A block of apartments was squeezed into the plot where once Mr. Weeks had lived. The only thing my grandfather could tell me about Mr. Weeks was that he was an elderly man who lived around the corner, and that he was a real gentleman. That didn't seem like much to remember, but it made an impression on my grandfather even after all these years.

We started for home eventually, and had almost reached it when we made one last detour. We turned into a little network of narrow streets that ended in dead ends, walled off from the through traffic.

"I wonder," said my grandfather, peering at the houses as he drove slowly past. "I was in one of these houses once, a long time ago. After we became engaged, your grandmother took me to a gathering around here, in one of these big houses. I didn't know anybody there. I wonder if I'd recognize the house."

"It doesn't look like they've torn anything down here, any-way."

"It was one of those two houses. That one, I think. Yes, that one. Still standing. It must have been fifty, almost sixty years ago."

My grandfather had stopped the car and was looking up at the big dark house. I looked too, trying to be companionable, but it didn't mean anything to me.

"There was a girl who played the harp. You didn't hear the harp much back then. I suppose you don't hear it much now. She had black hair, long black shiny hair." Then he shook his head. "I've kept you out long enough. Let's head home."

As we pulled away I kept looking back, expecting to see a face in the window. I thought I saw a curtain move on the first floor, but that was all.

3.

We went to church as a family too. We went to a Polish church around the corner, because it was close and because for a long while they were the only ones who still said a Mass in Latin. They also repeated the gospel in Polish, and sang Polish hymns, and made periodic announcements about various Polish festivals fea-turing exotic Polish delicacies, but that didn't bother us. Eventu-ally the parish got younger and the Polish content dropped and the Latin went with it, but by that time it had become a habit to go there.

That Sunday, we sat on the right side of the church about half-way up. My mother preferred to receive from a priest, so week to week she would move us around from left to right depending on where she thought the celebrant would be standing, but the priests were on to such games and used to mix it up to discourage gamblers. More and more they turned the whole thing over to their deputies, the Eucharistic ministers, so my mother finally accepted defeat and just took the most convenient open pew, though she would still cross lines when the opportunity presented itself.

When Mass had ended I was walking to the back of the church down the side aisle, but my sister seized me by the elbow and turned me around. She walked me up the aisle and led me out the side entrance.

"Mrs. Breen," she explained. "Talking to the parents."

I was grateful. Mrs. Breen was a grammar school teacher, whom I had always found to be an unusually insistent "pain in the tail" as my grandfather would have said. She taught me in the fourth grade, and I thought that it was understood that we had barely tolerated each other, but she had maintained an unseemly interest in my doings ever since. Many's the time she had waylaid my mother and me when we were out shopping on the main avenue. I thought that simple decency dictated that, after an interval of a few years, teachers and their former pupils should meet as strangers, but apparently Mrs. Breen didn't see it that way. I had done well in her class, and she had jumped to the conclusion that I was smart, and that I should do something with myself. I disagreed.

To make matters worse, when I tried to explain my position to my parents, my mother was moved to pity by my thorough but accurate and necessary catalog of the woman's flaws. She therefore extended all kindness to Mrs. Breen, and indulged her in conversation far beyond the modest demands of courtesy. So my sister had done me a favor.

We stood on the sidewalk by the side of the church. People were walking away in all directions, some cutting across the street to the parking lot on the other side.

"Did you see them?" My sister nodded to a knot of people already at the end of the block, about to cross the street "catty cornered," as we say. "I've never seen them before."

I could see, at the center of the group, a woman in a long white dress and a short blue jacket, with bright blonde hair and sharp-heeled shoes. She walked with authority and the others arranged themselves around her. Even at this distance, and from behind, I could she was something splendid. Walking next to her, taller even in flat shoes, stooping a little as if she was listening to the other talk, was my girl with the fuzzy hair. I recognized her at once. There were two men walking behind them, and I couldn't quite figure them out. They were obviously with the others, but walked behind at a respectful distance. They had very short hair, and wore dark coats that appeared at this distance to be identical. They were both smoking. They seemed to be in casual conversation, but never stopped scanning the road on both sides. One turned around once, and took a long look back. He saw me watching, and my sister and I got an unhurried stare that took us both in thoroughly. I stared back. I wasn't sure what I thought of him. He looked like a serious person.

They moved off, toward the little maze of dead end streets, where my grandfather and I had been the day before.

"That's an odd family," said my sister. "Nobody looks like the others, but they all look alike." She liked observing people; she always saw more than I did. We were both forever on the lookout for signs, omens, anything unusual, anything that would change our luck. We liked attributing great importance to trivialities. I did not tell her that I had seen the fuzzy-haired girl before, though.

We took up a position along our usual route home and waited for my parents and grandfather to catch up.

"Where were you?" asked my mother. "We were talking to Mrs. Breen."

"We saw her," said my sister darkly. "She's going to have to be a lot faster than that."

"Oh, you shouldn't be like that."

Maybe not, but we were.

"Gather us all, so old and boring," sang my sister.

"All right, all right."

"I'm not making fun of the music, I'm making fun of Mrs.

Breen by *means* of the music."

My father had just recently declared a moratorium on complaints and criticism after Mass. My grandfather had spurred the change when he overheard my sister and me on the walk home, gleefully critiquing what we considered willful and unpardonable liberties in the priest's performance of his duties, aided by my sister's gift for mimicry. He was dismayed.

"Gee, that's a hell of an attitude after Mass," he said. "It's ungrateful, really."

"They're imitating us," said my father. "That's all we do, complain. Everything given to us and no gratitude. That's just what the world needs, more complainers. We should all just give it a rest." Then, because he knew we needed it, he raised a forefinger and produced one of his aphorisms: "Resentment is an addiction. Left unchecked, it will devour reason."

So the family turned over a new leaf, and kept our "negative thoughts" to ourselves, at least on the way home, although sometimes I did notice my mother silently glaring at the ground. At first it was awkward, but we got used to it. We found other things to talk about.

4.

I had a plan for that afternoon. I wanted to find this fuzzy-haired girl and her companions and I thought I knew where to look. From the route her little group took after church, I figured that she lived in my grandfather's dead-end maze of the other day. Of course it was possible that they were going for a car, but I didn't think it likely. She probably lived close, since she rode her bicycle around the neighborhood. Also, you can usually tell if people are walking for a car, or walking to walk, and I thought it was the latter. You can tell a lot about people from the way they walk.

When I finished my sandwich, though, and got ready to go there was a knock at the door. I feared a stranger with pamphlets or a clipboard, but when I pulled the door open I saw my cousin standing before me.

"DT, what up?" he said.

"Troll! What are you doing here?" For he lived out on the Island.

He had given me the nickname DT, and it did not mean the usual. It stood for "Distant Third," and I had earned it in a foot race years ago. He started by using the full name, then shortened it to "Distant" or occasionally "Third" pronounced Irish-style without the "h" when he wanted to make a point, but finally he settled on the initials.

He had given himself the nickname Troll when we were all on vacation a couple of years back. Our families would sometimes go to a lake and rent a few cabins together. We would spend a week swimming and eating ice cream. We were standing waist deep in water one day when he began to pooch his stomach out.

"Look at that gut," he said proudly. "How does a guy my age get a gut like that? You know what I want to look like? One of those troll dolls."

He had short, thick arms and legs, so the potential was there. He was growing his hair long that year, and ducked his head down into the water, then popped up again and twisted his hair into a peak on the top of his head. We both burst out laughing. Later, he contrived to thicken the mass using sand and walked around with this sort of congealed flame at the top of his head for the rest of the day, which included dinner in a crowded diner. His persona as Troll was set. The hair was gone now, but Troll he remained.

"I need to use your bathroom," he said, and barged past me.

While he was in there, his mother, my Aunt Joanne, came up the steps and explained to my mother and me that they were looking for a used car for my cousin, and had followed up an advertisement in the neighborhood. They had just looked at the car, and thought they'd look in on us, since they were only a few minutes away.

"*You're* going to drive?" my sister was at the top of the stairs, and she leaned over the banister and addressed this question to my cousin who had just rejoined us.

"That's right, no more dangling from the rear view for me.

Heigh-ho-the-derio the Troll takes a car."

"We haven't bought it yet," his mother said, but I thought Troll would probably get his car. If not, it wouldn't matter. I liked and admired my cousin. I never saw him really bothered by anything. He seemed invulnerable, as a Troll should be.

We played ping pong for the rest of the afternoon. We had a table in the basement, and I was pretty good. Troll was good at everything, despite his unprepossessing physique. I liked playing with him. He never complained, never alibied. He won, he lost. He played. He didn't care. He was Troll.

It was late when they left, but they couldn't stay for supper. It was damp and getting cold when I wheeled my bicycle out of the garage. I had homework after dinner; already school was beginning to weigh on my mind. I rode through a few puddles to hear the sound of the water and watch the traces of the wet wheels. The church parking lot was empty of cars and some kids were playing roller hockey in it. They had brought their own net. I wandered through the dead end streets for a while. They were crowded. Most houses had more than one car, and many of them were thick heavy SUVs. The blue recycle bins were out by the curb, too. I didn't see any people. I kept backtracking and circling.

I was ready to give up, turning at the end of the last street, just a block away from the house my grandfather had shown me, when I heard a cat mewing. I looked up the nearest driveway and saw a girl come out the side door with a saucer. She came down the steps and bent to the cat, which quickly ran forward and buried its face in the milk. It was a young cat, dark grey, and the girl stroked it as it drank. She looked up and saw me watching her. I had stopped my bicycle in the street. Turnabout is fair play, I guess.

She stood up. She didn't seem surprised.

"Hello," she said.

"Hello."

"I saw you in church. Was that your family?"

"Yes. Was that yours?"

She considered.

"Yes," she said at length. "We live here. I live here with my aunt."

"Is that your cat?"

"No, it's a stray. It's only just past being a kitten, poor thing." She nodded towards my bicycle. "Do you like riding bikes? I do too. You should come over some time and we could go riding."

"Sure. I get home from school late though, during the week. After five."

"Why so late?"

"I have to take a bus. It's kind of a pain. When do you get home from school?"

"I don't go to school."

"Really? Never?"

"Never darken the door."

"Wow…that's great!"

"Yeah, we think so."

"That's really great…"

I didn't know what else to say. Envy is unseemly.

"Maybe I could come by on Saturday. To ride bikes, I mean."

"I'll be around. Unless I'm off on an errand."

"I live right near here. I can just swing by." Then I added, "How do you manage it? Not going to school I mean. Doesn't your aunt mind?"

The girl pushed out her lower lip and shook her head.

"She'd be the last person…"

Then I heard a voice calling from inside the house.

"Cornelia! It's finished. Bring it over to your cousin."

A woman was at the side door; I could see her silhouette against the light. She pushed the swinging door open and came out on the little landing.

"Tell him it's got to be done now, and to the letter."

Then she saw me.

"Well." She smiled at me. It was the woman from church, in the same white dress. She was in her bare feet now. They must have been cold on the brick.

"Hello. Cornelia, who is your friend?"

"I'm James Ward. I live in the neighborhood. Or not too far away."

"I'm pleased to meet you."

She descended half way down the steps, and extended her hand. I tipped my bicycle over in the driveway and hurried forward. I reached up. Her hand was small and soft but her grip was strong. For some reason I found her steady gaze overwhelming.

"I am Miss Vivien Widdershins. I am Cornelia's aunt."

I didn't know where to look. Every place seemed fraught with danger. Finally I took refuge in her eyes again.

"You must come visit Cornelia," she said kindly. "We would be glad to have you. Come next week or whenever you're free from school. But now, I am afraid, Cornelia has pressing business."

She handed a fat envelope to the girl. There was writing on the front, in thick blue strokes.

The girl took the letter without a word. She had an odd expression, her mouth wry as if she was making game of someone in her mind. Me, I supposed.

She gave the cat a last pat on the head.

"Gotta go," she said to no one in particular. She tucked the envelope inside her jacket, and hauled her bicycle out from behind the stoop. I did not think to ride with her. Her aunt watched her go, then turned to me.

"Well, good-bye," she said. "We will be seeing you soon, I hope."

I rode home in the gathering dark. They would be seeing me, I thought, as soon as I could manage. I don't know what this is, but it is something.

2. The House

I thought about them both a great deal throughout the week. While I was sitting on our school bus at eight o'clock in the morning looking through the rattling window at the grey neighborhoods, I thought of the girl at home, and of all those lovely free mornings and afternoons.

The freshmen were the low men on the bus totem pole. I was lucky because I was far enough away from school and early enough on the route that I always found an empty seat. Some of those who came aboard afterwards had to stand, and had to endure the ingenious torments of bored upperclassmen. The seniors were beyond such things; when they interfered it was only to ensure that certain standards were upheld, and often on behalf of the freshmen against their enemies. I was mostly left alone. My detachment baffled would-be persecutors. There were easier marks.

I don't remember what I learned in class. I went to a good school, I got good grades, I did not trouble my teachers. My father had taught me that work was the curse of Adam, so I pitied the poor working stiffs and tried to make things easy on them. It was a formality, an unpleasant ritual we all had to fulfill, but it meant nothing to me.

All that week I thought of the girl with the long nose, pedaling around on her bicycle, running errands for her aunt, for Miss Widdershins. I thought about the aunt, and memory failed. When I tried to remember what she looked like, detail escaped me. I remembered the white dress, the white skin, the silhouette, the pale bare feet. When I had looked at her that day I saw everything at once, but nothing by itself clearly. If someone had asked me, I could not have described her.

I had been worrying about time lately. Even at that early age, I knew that my time was running out fast, and had been since the day I was born. How many really good days had there been? Eight years wasted in grammar school, now four more in high school, and four more after that in college. All that time gone forever, with no hope of recovery. They were the Thieves of Time, I thought, as I listened to my poor teachers drone on and on in class.

That Friday was the Bad Assembly. I wrote it down in my diary. We had assemblies once a month or so, when the entire school gathered. There was always some reason – a speaker, a student band, a pep rally. I don't even remember what this one was about. I liked to get out of class, but you had to be careful where you sat. On this one occasion, my friend Trey and I were not careful, and we paid the price. There were two sophomores behind us, two mean sophomores, two sophomores who knew us.

In my father's day, assemblies were held in the gym, and the kids had to sit on the roll-out gym seating, with somebody's knees in your back as likely as not. Things had improved to some extent; they had built a new thousand-seat theater, and assemblies were held there, in comfortable theater seats, with a lot more chance to preserve one's personal space from intrusion. My father had been disgusted by this extravagant outlay of money. He never donated money to his alma mater. I agreed with him in theory, but I was glad for the margin of safety. I went to an all-boys school, which had some advantages supposedly. They were never convincingly explained to me.

The two sophomores behind us were discussing the manifold negative characteristics displayed by my friend and myself, and trying to develop a theory to explain them. They were Heyward and Tucci, one black and one white, and they explored our worthlessness from a racial perspective.

"You're letting me down, Wilson," said Heyward. "I mean, most brothers have got something to recommend them, but you got nothing. I mean you're little and ugly and dumb. Give me something…help me out here."

"He dresses OK," said Tucci, generously. "Look at Ward. He

looks like a country boy come to the big city for the first time. Don't you have anything that fits?"

"But Wilson wears the same thing every day. I mean every damn day."

"I never noticed that."

"It's pitiful. Isn't Ward supposed to be smart?"

"Him? Please, he's an idiot."

Trey looked sidelong at me through narrowed eyes.

"I hate sophomores," he said. "Hate them. Juniors and seniors at least are grown, but sophomores are only halfway there so they think they have something to prove."

Heyward's voice took on a new tone. He had elected to take offense.

"Oh...my...goodness! Oh my goodness me."

We turned around to see Heyward and Tucci exchange thunderstruck looks.

"Did he just call me a half man? Is that what he did?"

"It sounded that way to me," said Tucci helpfully.

"Is that what you did? Did you call me a half man?"

"Take it the way you take it."

"Is that what you said?"

"Take it the way you take it." Trey clung to his phrase. He disdained explanation.

"Oh, there will be retribution for this. Severe retribution." Heyward leaned forward and spoke in Trey's ear. "This is way too big for assembly. So relax, man. Nothing will happen to you here. This is way too big for assembly. Relax. Enjoy the show. But it's coming."

"You won't know when." Tucci was still helping out.

"That's right. You won't know when. You won't know where. But you'll know it when it comes. The wheels of justice turn slowly, my friend. But they turn."

True to their words, they did not bother us for the rest of the assembly. On our way out, though, as we waited in line to go up the stairs, we saw them looking at us from across the hall. Heyward frowned, and nodded meaningfully at Trey, and rolled his dense fists past each other, indicating the "wheels of justice."

That gave us something to think about. Ours was not the kind of school where people got knifed. There were no gangs. We even had a dress code: jackets and ties. We were not in real danger, but they could make things unpleasant for us, and our freshman imaginations were ready to supply much of what reality lacked.

2.

I rode the bus home that evening through a light mist of rain, the kind I usually like. I worried about the weather that day, though, staring out the window as all around me my schoolmates pecked away at their electronics. It looked like it could get worse. It did not look like bicycle weather.

In my father's day, there was mayhem on the bus, or so he said. "The Vice" was the chief form of warfare. The assailant would put both feet against the two opposite seats and use his legs to push his victim against the side of the bus and sometimes against the window. The best defense was a headlock or chokehold of some description, what they call now a "Rear Naked Choke," if you could pull it off. If others piled on, there was nothing for it but endurance. One year, there were enough broken seats and broken windows that the whole busload of students was called before the Headmaster to endure group punishment and disgrace. The Queens Bus became something of a legend in those days. My father, a peaceful man himself, seemed oddly disappointed to hear that the violence had stopped. Another tradition lost to technology.

I got off the bus into the icy drizzle. I was wearing a big pea jacket, which I had selected in the hope that it would make me look somewhat nautical and even a bit rough and ready. It did not. I looked like a little kid in a big kid's coat. It was warm though and had a high collar, and gave off an unpleasant but interesting scent of lanoline when it got wet.

My book bag felt light when I slung it over my shoulder. I realized that I had left my massive biology text in my locker. There was an important assignment due on Monday. I stood on the sidewalk, thinking. Whom could I call? From whom could I borrow the book? Then I pulled myself together. This was a test. I would simply not do the assignment and explain that I forgot the book. What could they do to me? Dock my grade? Fail me? "Don't let them worry you." I could hear my father. "Never let them see you sweat." It was advice I needed, since I was very much given to fretting. This would be a good training exercise.

The avenue was busy. It was rush hour and I unfocused my eyes and allowed myself to be pleasantly dazzled by the white, yellow and red lights shining on the slick dark road. Most of the streets along my route were residential, but there were a couple of blocks with stores and businesses that were always crowded at this hour. People had to double park to get their grocery shopping done, and the traffic had to find a way to squeeze past. People were always more impatient in the rain.

Two men stepped out of a butcher shop a few doors ahead of me, and I snapped out of my ambulatory daze. They were the two bodyguards I had seen with Miss Widdershins and Cornelia after Sunday mass. Bodyguards. That's what they had reminded me of! They still wore identical dark coats and their identical round close-cropped heads were bare to the rain. They both carried many packages. I picked up my pace and slipped in behind them, hoping to overhear some of their conversation.

One of them nodded toward the little liquor store.

"Better pick up some cognac."

"We've got cognac."

"She wants more."

"Well, the Colonel likes his cognac."

The other laughed.

"He's not the only one."

"When are they coming?"

"Who knows? Soon."

"Not before the Rhymer, *ta sulam*."

"We better pick up some single malt, too."

"Aquavitae!" proclaimed the other stopping before the door, and they both walked into the store.

I knew now why they had looked so similar from afar. They were twins. I didn't know what they were talking about, but I knew who "she" was, and I saw that, like Cornelia, they seemed to do what she said. I suspected that a lot of people did.

I couldn't follow them into the liquor store, so I continued homeward, looking back every once in a while. It began raining harder, and I realized that I had forgotten my umbrella on the bus. My mother would tell me to check the Lost and Found, but I knew I'd never see the umbrella again. A pretty poor day all around.

But after dinner, we made popcorn and gathered to watch a *Rockford Files* episode. My father bought the DVDs season by season, and we watched them methodically, creating an alternate TV schedule with these and other favorites. It was a good episode, an Angel episode. The day ended well, and when I woke up the next morning, the sun was shining.

3.

It was not until after lunch that I managed to pedal out to Miss Widdershins' place. My grandfather took it into his head to clear away all the dead branches and twigs from around our house that morning, and my mother insisted that I help him. She worried about him tottering around alone with shears and a tree saw. There had been mishaps in the past.

It felt strange to be riding over to visit Cornelia. It was unlike me to seek acquaintance with anyone. Avoidance was my normal response to other people. I sometimes wondered if I was autistic. There was a lot of talk about autism in those days. Supposedly there was a "spectrum" of autism. Might I not be somewhere on it?

When I got to Miss Widdershins' house I wheeled my bicycle up the walk and leaned it against the left front railing. Her house was very unusual in that it still had a screened-in front porch. Most of the other porches in the neighborhood had long ago been closed off and converted into rooms. I climbed the steps and raised my hand to knock when I saw through the screen a figure rise. A man had been seated in a chair by the inside front door.

"Can I help you?" he asked, and swung the screen door outward a quarter turn.

It was one of the bodyguards, still wearing his coat. It must have been cold waiting there by the door.

"I'm here to see Cornelia."

"Cornelia? Is she expecting you? Oh, yes, I remember, you're the fellow with the bicycle. Ward. Come in, I'll call her."

I stepped into the dark porch. There were some garden chairs lined up against the inside wall, but not much else.

The bodyguard popped his head inside the house.

"Get Cornelia," he said. "Her friend is here."

Then he turned back to me.

"Have a seat," he said. "They'll find her."

He resumed his chair by the door and picked up a cigar that had been left balancing on the arm.

I looked at him sidelong. He had a hard face, I thought. Not mean, but hard. Again, I thought he looked foreign. There was a layer of fat, of softness, of easy living, that I had come to expect that just was not there.

The inside door opened and I rose, but it was not Cornelia. A man appeared, a small man who placed his feet carefully, as if from a habit of deference. He seemed pleased though, as he looked about him.

"You look happy," remarked the bodyguard.

"I am. It's a good day."

He started to say more, but then saw me and fell silent.

"I'm glad," the bodyguard patted him kindly on the shoulder.

"*Ban wassail ee*," said the little man, or something like it, and he was off down the steps.

Before the bodyguard could sit again, the inside door flipped open and Cornelia hopped out onto the porch.

"You made it!" she said. "I wasn't sure you'd come."

"Can you go for a ride?"

"Sure, Aunt Vivien is busy all day anyway."

"What's she doing?" I wasn't usually nosy but I was intrigued.

Cornelia waved one hand about in an expansive manner, as she groped for the words.

"Helping people," she said at last.

The bodyguard said nothing as we left, just returned to his cigar and his seat.

I had to ask.

"Who is he?"

"The doorman."

Soon we were pedaling down the street. Cornelia didn't seem particular as to where we went, or how fast we got there. I had a fondness for odd places like the backs of store rows where businesses laid out their trash and the garages behind garden apartments, places people couldn't see from the main street. I took her to a footpath that dipped under the Long Island Railroad overpass where the tracks crossed the Expressway. We could watch the train cross overhead, while the cars roared by alongside us. She seemed to find this interesting. Neither one of us spoke much.

It was not an especially cold day, but it was still March, and eventually my hands began to turn blue where they clutched the handlebars. The tip of Cornelia's nose was red, and she began to sniff a little.

"Do you want to head back?"

"Yeah. I have to read some French anyway."

"I thought you didn't go to school."

"Aunt Vivien is teaching me French. Let's go by your house on the way, I want to see where you live."

When we got to my house she stopped pedaling and coasted past, looking up. She took a couple of turns in the road, while I slowed to a crawl, balancing. I saw my sister gazing out the front window at us, curiously. I didn't want to stop. Cornelia pushed on eventually and we were soon wheeling up to her aunt's house. They really only lived a few blocks away.

Cornelia invited me into the house. The bodyguard was still waiting on the porch, but he was standing and stretching, as if his day was finished. He opened the inner door to let us both in, and then followed us inside.

I looked around curiously. I got the impression of a lot of wood. There were no rugs. The floors were of dark wide wood boards, worn smooth over years. It seemed like a quiet house. It seemed that they had just moved in and might move out at any moment. Before I could take in any details, I heard the stairs creak, and saw Miss Widdershins descending.

"That's the last of them, I think," she said. She held in her hands an enormous wad of money that she was shuffling through, dividing, rearranging. I couldn't see the denominations, but I thought it must run into thousands.

She looked up and saw me with Cornelia.

"Oh, hello," she said. "I'm glad you could pay us a visit. Did you have an enjoyable ride?"

"Yes," said Cornelia. "It's cold though. Is there anything warm to drink?"

"There's a pot of tea. It should still be warm."

She walked over to the bodyguard, peeled off a good slab of bills and laid it in his hand. He pocketed it with a quick nod of acknowledgment.

"Put the rest in the box."

He took the remainder and walked out of the room with it. Cornelia called in from the other room.

"Do you take milk or sugar?"

I didn't drink tea at all. I picked milk.

"Bring one in for me, too."

"I have to warm it up a bit."

I was left alone with Miss Widdershins. She took her seat on a couch and stretched out her legs, crossing them at the ankle. She favored long dresses; this one was blue. Her black high-heeled boots only just cleared the skirt.

"Sit, sit," she said waving me into a chair. She looked at me with interest.

"Cornelia says you're teaching her French," I said.

"As well as I can. My conversation is poor. I remember the grammar well enough."

"Have you ever been to France?"

"Do they teach you languages at your school?"

"I'm taking German. And Latin."

"Latin!" she seemed pleased. "Very good. I didn't know they still taught that."

"I think it's coming back. But my school has always taught Latin. My father went there when he was a boy."

She nodded.

"You are first year, yes?"

"Yes, I'm a freshman."

I heard the kettle start to whistle inside and then subside to a hiss when it was taken off the burner. Cornelia was warming the pot. I could hear her clinking around with the cups and creamer. Sound carried well in the house; it must be all the bare wood.

Miss Widdershins gazed out the window. She didn't seem to mind silence. I took the time to peek at her. She had high cheekbones and smooth pale skin. I thought her eyes might be small, but very keen. Her hair was thick and yellow and magnificent. She was not thin.

Cornelia glided in with a tray. She passed from one of us to the other.

"Milk for James, milk for Aunt Vivien, and sugar lumps for Cornelia."

She curled up on the other end of the couch from her aunt. I sipped cautiously at my tea.

The bodyguard reappeared.

"I'll be off now, if you don't need me."

"Certainly. Oh, piece of news. Thomas is in town. Watch the tea, Cornelia! I thought you'd be pleased."

"Good," said the bodyguard. "That will be a help. Any word on the Colonel?"

"No change. But he won't be here before our lot."

"Good, good. Good news all around." Then, tossing "so long," over his shoulder, he was out the front door.

"When is Uncle Tom coming here?"

"Within the fortnight."

"Why so long?"

"He's on business. Never you mind what business, girl."

"I know what business."

Miss Widdershins shook her head in a deliberate manner and Cornelia lapsed into silence briefly.

"James is learning Latin, too, at his school."

"*Is ea id, eius eius eius*," Cornelia recited rapidly.

"Perhaps you can correspond in Latin. For practice."

"Really, Aunt Vivien!" Cornelia rolled her eyes.

"No, perhaps not."

They both laughed. We made small talk over tea, something I had never done before. Miss Widdershins sat very straight and calm. Cornelia, her feet tucked beneath her, could barely sit still. At length, Miss Widdershins' eyes drifted to the window.

"It's getting dark," she said. "Your parents will be expecting you home."

We all rose, and Cornelia saw me to the screen door.

"Wait'll you meet my Uncle Tom," she said. "He's my ma's brother. He's my favorite. Aunt Vivien's, too," she added with a wink. "Beware the Ides of March," she added as a valedictory remark and let the door slam.

4.

Miss Widdershins was right, my parents had been expecting me. I had been out a long time for a bicycle ride on a cold day. My mother was a worrier, and pressed me with questions.

"I was at a friend's house," I said finally.

"A friend? What friend?"

"Was it that waif I saw you with?" asked my sister. "James was with a waif."

"What are you talking about?"

"James was riding his bicycle in the company of a waif."

"What waif?"

"She looked like a nice waif."

So I had to explain.

"I don't like you going into strange houses."

"It wasn't that strange."

"James, I'm serious. We don't know these people. I don't like you being fed by strangers. There are a lot of nuts in the world. People get abducted all the time."

"They go to St. Stanislaus. They were there last week."

My mother made a sound between a sniff and a snort. "Lots of people go to church. What's their address?"

"I don't know. I could find it again, though."

"What's their phone number?"

"I don't know."

"I don't like it."

I decided not to argue, and to let my mother get used to the idea. I'd let her talk it over with my father. I had left out the bits about the bodyguard, and the clients, and the wads of cash. It was difficult to put an innocent interpretation on any of it. I didn't worry about it, though. I lay awake that night thinking about Miss Widdershins' black boots with the silver buckles, crossed at the ankle, and her perfect posture under her long blue dress. Maybe I would see them tomorrow in church, I thought.

3. The Tribes

1.

We didn't see the Widdershins group on Sunday. Probably they had gone to an earlier mass. My sister took Monday off to go to the St. Patrick's Day Parade; I took the day off too, but stayed home. My father encouraged us to take days off on such occasions. He wrote the required notes for us.

We used to worry about it.

"We're not supposed to take off unless we're sick," we would say.

My father would bark in derision.

"What are you going to tell them?"

"I'm going to tell them I decided to keep you home."

"But we're not supposed to..."

"I'm your father. I decided to keep you home. End of story. If they don't like it, tell them to call me."

But they never did.

My father took a personal day from work. He pulled out his old records from the seventies: The Chieftains, The Bothy Band, Seamus Ennis, the whole crew. We still had a turntable. He listened in contentment for a while, then he took out his fiddle and began to play. I think he might have been good once, but he only played now once in a great while. I think he must have played with others once, too, but now he played alone. On this day, though, my Aunt Kate stopped over to bring us some bread she'd baked. She had left one of her old flutes in my grandfather's closet, and when she heard my father playing, she brought down the wooden box, and carefully screwed the old instrument together. With a great deal of noisy breathing down the pipe to warm it up, she got it going again. She had studied classical flute, not traditional, so she

34

played mostly airs and songs. She and my father played together old favorites that they hadn't played for years. They stumbled together over all the old familiar places. It made my grandfather happy to hear them again, but Aunt Kate had to cut the afternoon short. She had to pick up my two cousins from school.

"You see?" asked my father, looking at me in an accusatory manner. "School."

I saw.

It was not a good week. When I did return to school on Tuesday, I was truly a day late and a dollar short. I was already overdue with my biology assignment, which I hadn't even begun. That price had to be paid in full. It was a long assignment, designed for a weekend, and it kept me up very late on Tuesday and Wednesday nights. I made a poor job of it, even before the late penalties, but I finished. I couldn't get any sleep even when I did get to bed, because there was a full moon out, and that always unsettled my rest. Everyone was unsettled that week. The news was full of the rumor of war. Most people seemed happy, and the kids at school discussed advanced weapons systems with great confidence. My mother was upset. My father's remarks during his news programs were angrier and more sarcastic than ever, but he sat through them alone and spoke to the screen. My grandfather stayed away, sitting in the living room and reading Wordsworth.

I was glad when the weekend finally rolled around again, but I was still faced with the problem of how to accustom my mother to the idea of me visiting the Strange House. I had been preoccupied over the week, and hadn't laid any groundwork. As it happened, Cornelia solved my problem by simply showing up at our front door early Saturday afternoon.

My mother's world view was strongly colored by the constant warnings she received on television, on radio and in magazines – warnings about crime, health hazards, terrorism, dangers of all descriptions – which she took quite seriously. Fortunately, however, the personal always took priority with her. Once she met someone, and took a liking to him, it didn't matter what the warnings were: he was in. As far as I know, she was never wrong about anyone. She took an instant liking to Cornelia, and my problem was solved. There would be no more talk about me going to strange houses.

I was sitting in our porch, watching TV. It was filler, some sports show about top high school athletes around the country. This one was about a tall blonde female volleyball player who impressed me a great deal. She was from somewhere out in California, where such fabled creatures arose. I wondered again why I went to an all-boys school. My mother walked in and announced, in a somewhat conspiratorial manner, that there was a friend at the front door asking for me.

I found Cornelia standing just inside the door. She looked tentative, as if she was trying not to press the boards too hard.

"I had to leave the house. Things are crazy over there. Do you want to go down to the park?"

My mother pressed food on her, as she always did when people crossed our threshold. Cornelia held out for a time, but finally agreed to a glass of orange juice. She sat sipping at our kitchen counter, and wrapped her thin denim-clad legs around the high metal chair. Her hair was pulled behind her in a great mass. She seemed like a captive woodland creature. My mother was enchanted by her, and she seemed to reciprocate. I even learned that her full name was Cornelia Parsons.

We talked for a good long while; Cornelia seemed reluctant to leave. I was proud of my mother, because she did not pry, as many another would.

When we set off at last, I was surprised to see that Cornelia had come on foot. She had long legs and an easy stride that covered ground deceptively fast. She walked us past the public school where I went to kindergarten, and past the public tennis courts where I had once made an effort to learn tennis. I didn't stick with it for some reason. I wasn't bad, and I wasn't good either. I didn't exactly lose interest; I just sort of drifted away.

I could tell Cornelia about the local landmarks, but when we got to the park itself, she returned the favor. She seemed to have an intimate knowledge of the animal life that made its home there.

Rabbits, raccoons, possums, owls...she knew where they lived, when they came out of hiding, when they went back to sleep.

"Do you want to go down to the bay and look for rats?" she asked brightly.

I liked to go down by the water, though I had never thought of the rats as much of an attraction. My father said that there was a time, in the early nineties, when the park used to be crawling with them once the sun went down. When he walked along the path overlooking the bay at dusk, he would amuse himself by counting their dim shapes as they scurried off into the long grass. The park was well kept now, but it used to be a very different place, he said. In the seventies, the benches were broken, the pagodas were burnt and painted with graffiti, and there was broken glass everywhere. My father remembered it all, era by era.

The park was separated from the water by a highway. You crossed over a wide footbridge, with a floor of boardwalk-style planks. I used to enjoy dragging my sneakers over the tough wood. When my sister and I were younger, we used to watch the cars rushing underneath, and pretend we were dodging them. If one crossed under you, you lost. It wouldn't have been much fun that day, because traffic was jammed in both directions. My father never drove on this road if he could help it.

We crossed the bridge and walked down the ramp to the concrete pathway that stretched along the bay. The tide was high. There were some kids fishing off the rocks; I can't imagine they caught anything. We dawdled along the path and poked among the big boulders that bordered the water. There was some mildly interesting detritus – a fence section with barbed wire attached, a wooden door, a broken oar – but no rats. I was neither surprised nor disappointed. We did see a trio of regal swans swim past, moving easily across the broken water. We watched in happy silence.

"Clan Lir," said Cornelia when they had passed.

"What?"

"The Children of Lir."

I nodded sagely, resolving to look it up when I got home.

At length we turned back toward the land. We had just started climbing the ramp, when I heard a voice calling loudly from one of the stopped cars on the highway.

"Hey! Hey you! Yo!"

An idiot, I thought. One thing remained constant in New York, seventies, eighties, nineties, into the new millennium, always and forever: idiots. I kept walking.

"Yo, Ward, are you deaf?"

I turned sharply. This particular idiot knew me. I peered at the cars, then saw him sticking his head out of the rear window of a Camaro. It was Tucci. I was amazed. I remembered then that he lived in Queens, though he never took the bus.

"Your friend is dead!" he said. "Heyward is going to bury him. Tell him. Tell him he's finished." He started laughing maniacally and banging on the roof of the car with one hand. "He's a dead man!"

I saw heads wagging inside the car, and another idiot thrust his head out of the front window and gibbered at me.

The traffic picked up and they were swept away.

"Who was that?" Cornelia asked. "Is he crazy?"

"No, he's a sophomore. He's someone from my school. I can't believe we ran into him out here. I've never seen him outside school before."

"Who was he talking about? Who is dead?"

"It's nothing really." I explained the situation to her. I wasn't sure what she made of it. What did she know of assemblies, sophomores, and the code we all lived by?

She grasped the essential.

"So you're not in any danger? Nor your friend."

"No, not really. It's all just a dumb joke."

She nodded seriously.

"Good."

Something about the way she said it caught my attention. She hadn't sounded alarmed, just…helpful. What if Trey and I had been in danger? I thought suddenly of the bodyguard sitting before Miss Widdershins' door. I watched Cornelia surreptitiously as she moved placidly along. She had dropped into my life as easily as if we were old friends, but I didn't really know anything about her.

She broke into a sudden giggle.

"The Wheels of Justice," she said.

"Yeah, pretty dramatic."

2.

We didn't say much the rest of the way, just walked back in contentment. She brought us a long way around, and I realized that we were headed to Miss Widdershins' house. I was dragging; it was a long walk. She led us up a back way, first squeezing between two fences, then balancing on top of a brick wall. I didn't much like crossing other people's property, but I didn't say anything.

"Don't worry," she said, "they're never home over the weekends."

We came up behind Miss Widdershins' garage, and up her driveway. I heard voices; it sounded like a farewell. I let Cornelia lead the way along the driveway; she moved cautiously over the gravel.

"Convey my regards to the Colonel. Tell him I will read what he sent us. I'm sorry I have nothing of the kind to send back to him, but as you know this is all unexpected. Well, I hope to see you soon. Better days for the Regiment," and she added, "*layanta is far*," or something that sounded like it.

We were far enough toward the front of the house that we could just peek around the corner. There were two men on the walk at the foot of the front steps. I could guess Miss Widdershins was standing on the stairs. The men had drooping moustaches and long hair that made them look like desperadoes.

I saw a shapely white arm extend itself toward them, and both men bent forward to kiss the hand in turn. Then they saluted, literally, turned and walked away.

Miss Widdershins watched them in silence, until they were out of earshot.

"Well, that's that." She said. "It buys us some time, but I never like to see our cousins in difficulty."

"Tommy should be here in a few days." I recognized the voice of one of the bodyguards.

"He should be here now. Everything's getting more difficult nowadays, it takes twice as long to get anything done. Extra care must be taken. That reminds me, did you notice when we were inside? They both had tattoos. MacOwen lets his people get tattooed now?"

"They get them when they're in service."

"It's a distinguishing mark. Dadda always said that was bad policy."

"All those Bellymen get tattoos now anyway. College kids and shopkeepers, businessmen and barflies. The butcher, the baker, the candlestick maker. It gets so you don't even notice it."

"A distinguishing mark," Miss Widdershins repeated. "Triple fleur-de-lis on one and ivy wreath on the other. Why make it easier for people? Hello, Cornelia, aren't you going to come round and greet us?"

"I didn't want to butt in." Cornelia led me around the corner.

"They're gone now. It's all off. The Regiment had to call it off. They've got too many people called up on active duty. Hello, James, you look tired. Has Cornelia worn you out?"

Miss Widdershins was spectacular. She wore a long white dress, cunningly embroidered, that emphasized her figure. Her hair was pushed back by some kind of beret that looked to be gold. One was tempted to call it a tiara. She wore a black locket on a gold chain that I didn't dare look at closely. There were heavy rings on the fingers of both her hands.

I must have answered something.

"Cornelia's a dangerous person for walking. I've learned not to let her take the lead."

"Wow, Aunt Vivian, you look tremendous."

"Thank you, sweetie. I put on the regalia today. All for naught, as it happens. I'd better get inside."

We followed them in. Both bodyguards were there. They had both shaved, so it appeared they were going formal as well. By the time we got inside, one of them had brought Miss Widdershins a short blue jacket which she was buttoning on.

"You two go into the kitchen and help yourselves to something."

3.

It was not a suggestion. When we got in the little room, even smaller than my kitchen at home, Cornelia wanted to make hot chocolate. I watched her rip the packets and stir them into the warming milk.

"Boy, Aunt Vivien sure dresses up nice. Too bad Uncle Tom wasn't here."

"Is he her husband?"

"Nope. Wants to be."

I must have looked at her quizzically.

"Aunt Vivien isn't really my aunt. She's my first cousin once removed. She's my father's cousin. Uncle Tom, on the other hand, really is my uncle. He's my mother's brother."

I nodded.

"Different families."

I nodded again.

"Aunt Vivien is a Dragon," Cornelia enunciated.

I looked up at her, but she was gazing into the saucepan, swirling the spoon.

"What do you mean?"

"What they call themselves. The Dragons. We all came over the ocean a long time ago. We stuck together. We stayed our own thing. We're kind of a tribe, with our own laws."

"Like gypsies?"

"Kind of like gypsies. We've got a lot of different families. You must have noticed we were odd."

"I noticed something."

Cornelia was pouring the hot chocolate out into two mugs.

"The Dragons are the oldest. Aunt Vivien is the Queen of the Dragons. So she's the leader of us all."

She brought the cups over.

"Is that why they kiss her hands?"

"Yeah. Though I think they'd kiss them anyway. Wouldn't you?"

And Cornelia suddenly thrust her knuckles out toward me and raised her eyebrows imperiously. Before I could react, she had removed her hand back to her cup of hot chocolate, and sat snickering at the joke.

"So what about the Regiment? Are they part of it?"

"Yes."

"And what about the Bellymen? Who are they?"

Cornelia seemed surprised.

"Where did you hear about Bellymen?"

"One of the bodyguards."

"No. You're the Bellymen. That's one of our names for you people. No offense."

"None taken. What are some other names?"

"So you pegged the Twins as bodyguards."

"That's what they seem like."

"That's pretty much what they are. Or retainers. It's an hereditary office."

I thought about it. Cornelia sipped chocolate and watched me think.

"That's why you don't go to school."

"Correct. We don't do a lot of things other people do. And we do a lot of things other people don't. It varies some from family to family. The Regiment is more, um, more assimulated. They have to be."

"So what are you?"

"I'm a girl. No, I'm mixed. Most of us are. I grew up with the Cats, with my mama's people. Now I foster with the Dragons, with Aunt Vivien. It doesn't matter that much. We're all friends and relations." She paused. "We've been having a little trouble with the Regiment, though. There was supposed to be a big meeting, but that's all off. A lot of the Regiment are still in military service, so they are all in a tizzy because of the war."

"What sort of trouble?"

"They're not convinced Aunt Vivien should be leader. At least some of them aren't. MacOwen for one. There's nothing in it, though. Everyone will stand with Aunt Vivien."

"So MacOwen is chief of the Regiment?"

"Correct. Colonel, to be precise. The chief of the Regiment is always the Colonel. Since the old days."

She gazed into her hot chocolate for a while, then began singing meditatively:

'tis but a chance, for he's gone to France
To wear the fleur de lis

We sat in silence for a while. I enjoyed sitting in Miss Widdershins cozy bare kitchen, finishing off the last grounds of the chocolate. It felt like home.

Just as I finished up, Miss Widdershins appeared in the doorway in her tight blue jacket.

"Rested?"

It was time to go.

"Rested," I said and stood up.

Passing her in the doorway, I had a moment of doubt. Should I make some sign of respect? But she smiled and inclined her head in a way that made me feel that I must have made such a sign unawares. I did notice that she seemed taller. She must have put on a good pair of heels for the occasion. All part of the regalia, I supposed. Cornelia saw me off at the door as usual. This time she watched me walk away.

On my way home it occurred to me that she had not even bothered to tell me to keep all this stuff, all about the Dragons and the Regiment and Queen Aunt Vivien, to myself. She knew. They were that sure of me.

That was how Cornelia and I became regular visitors. I loved to go over to her house and bask in the golden presence of Miss Widdershins. Every time I went there was some new curiosity to enchant or puzzle me. It seemed they were still moving in, and I would find new paintings on the wall, a row of freshly burnt out candles dripping frozen wax across the mantelpiece, a carved dragon crest hammered above the outside doorway.

Cornelia liked to come to my house and sit on our floor and watch TV. My mother would come into the porch and bring her food and urge her to sit in a chair and make a fuss over her, and Cornelia would beam. We had the same taste in outdoor adventure, which was to make long expeditions that ended nowhere. We would wind up standing under a bridge watching the water lap, or pedaling round and round an empty schoolyard, or walking across the hot roof of a parking garage. There we would gaze about us without a word, and then at length turn around and make our way happily home. We were at one another's houses every free weekend, and when summer came, more often than that, and so we became tangled up in one another's families, which proved interesting for us both.

4. The Dragons

1.

It was at this time that I began to drift apart from my friend Trey. We did not argue, or even have a difference of opinion. He simply became absorbed in a new interest that left little time for anything else. He informed me in confidential tones, the very week after Cornelia had told me about the Dragons, that he had begun lifting weights. I didn't make much of it at first. It seemed like an innocent, or even admirable activity, but it soon became clear that this was no casual pastime. Our school day was arranged in such a way that we had one free period during the day. Trey and I, and a few other congenial souls, had usually contrived to spend that time together in almost perfect and perfectly enjoyable idleness. Now, Trey disappeared to the school's exercise room, so as not to let even a half hour go to waste. His conversation became monotonous, and to me impenetrable. What did I know about sets, drop sets, cheat curls, training to failure? I sometimes looked over in the one class we shared together, Latin, and saw him with his arm wrapped around himself in an odd embrace. I could see his hand pinching his back, feeling for incipient lat development. He was still his old agreeable self, he was simply obsessed. I found that, with him missing in action, I did not have quite so many friends as I thought I did. More and more, the school week became only an interlude between visits with Miss Widdershins and Cornelia.

It was clear to me, though Trey never said it, that his sudden interest in body building was a response to the incident at the assembly. He seemed to take it as a personal challenge in a way I couldn't really understand. He was a tough kid, I guess, and didn't like people pushing him around, or trying to. As for me, it didn't trouble me at all. So a couple of sophomores bothered us. That's what they're supposed to do. We all had our roles to play. I didn't take any of it personally.

Heyward, by some means, had discovered this new obsession of Trey's. He seized upon it with delight. He surprised us one day by walking over to our lunch table, standing opposite us, rolling up his right sleeve, and striking a biceps pose while emitting a fearsome grunt. He was a big strong kid, a wrestler, and he made a notable show. He finished by showering kisses on his biceps. A table of his friends watched us from afar and howled. Trey was unmoved.

"OK," he said. "OK. Wait a while."

Heyward soon improved his mockery by recruiting his wrestler friends. With increasing frequency we would be ambushed in the hallways, on the stairs, in the lunch room, even in the parking lot. We would hear Heyward's voice sing out in Teutonic accent, "Posedown!" and be confronted by a gesticulating, writhing, boiling mass of wrestlers, staring fixedly at Trey, striking every muscle pose known to man.

Trey was unmoved.

"Wait a while," he said.

Heyward addressed him now only in that accent.

"Ja, you know I think it's fantastic that you are working out, OK, because then it will be so much more satisfying when I crush you."

Trey was unmoved. But Trey was beginning to bore me.

They had lost interest in me. Tucci confronted me once, soon after surprising me and Cornelia by the bay.

"Who was that girl I saw you with? Was that your sister?"

"No."

"Is she a cousin?"

"No."

Tucci nodded and smirked.

"Stick with her, baby, she'll fill out."

It sounded nasty, but I took it as a signal that I was out of it, and so I was. I felt a little guilty, but it really wasn't up to me. I had other interests myself now, anyway. I suppose I was in the grip of my own obsession.

2.

I think it was two weeks after I first learned about the Dragons
and their peculiar institutions that I made the acquaintance of the
"Uncle Tom" I had been hearing about. Oddly enough, I didn't
enter that in my diary.

The three of them were sitting on the front steps, a living tab-
leau. Miss Widdershins was sitting at the top, on the landing, with
her white hands laid on the shoulders of a man I had never seen
before. He was a dark man, with shaggy hair that looked as if it
had been cut short and had grown out untended. He had nine-
teenth-century-looking whiskers down the side of his face that left
his lip and chin bare. He wore a long dark coat that spread on the
steps around him, and black boots. I was afraid of him. As long
as I knew him, he was never anything other than courteous, even
friendly, to me, but I was always afraid of him. To me, looking
at the yellow-haired Miss Widdershins seated at her ease behind
him, it seemed as though she was holding a tiger by the finest of
fine gold chains.

I didn't see Cornelia at first. I heard a voice address me from
near the ground.

"Greetings, James, say hello to Uncle Tom."

She was hanging by her legs from the railing. Her long curly
hair brushed the earth.

"Bear yourself more seemly, Cornelia," said her uncle, out
of the side of his mouth. He laid his glass on the steps next to
him, and arose to greet me. He was tall and gave an impression of
denseness, of solidity. When he shook my hand and I looked up
at his pale eyes, it seemed to me that I was gazing back through a
thousand years of warfare and strife. It was an unsettling vision.

"My name is Thomas Gregory. I am Cornelia's Uncle, as you
just heard."

"Hi. I'm James Ward."

Cornelia had dropped to the ground and was walking towards

us on her hands. We watched her approach. For all she was so skinny I always marveled at her strength. At length she began to pitch forward, and with an "alley oop" tucked into a roll and hopped to her feet.

"You have energy," the man commented.

"Yes," said Cornelia warily.

"Would you like to help your old uncle out?"

"Maybe."

He handed her his empty glass.

"Before you go off on your escapade."

"Och." She took the glass and climbed into the house. "Come on Jamie."

I looked around hungrily for new features as I always did when I entered Miss Widdershins' house. There was a new row of stout silver candlesticks arranged across the mantelpiece, keeping the melted wax off the wood.

Cornelia paused.

"Look at this," she said. "I want to show you something."

She started up the stairs. I hung back. I had always kept to the first floor.

"Come on," she said and made an impatient gesture with her head, leading upward. The stairs turned right halfway up, and led to a long dark hallway. I felt as if I were entering a sanctuary or some enchanted place. I walked as softly as I could. I even tried to breathe quietly. Cornelia had no such scruples and strode down the hall dangling the glass of beer by the handle and dripping bits of foam on the floor.

"This is my favorite painting anywhere," she said.

At the end of the hall, on a narrow expanse of white wall with doorways opening on either side, hung a small dark painting. We stood and gazed. Within a carved gilt frame darkened by long age, there showed a street scene from long ago, with perfectly fashioned red brick buildings and a cobblestone street. It was mostly dark, shading almost to black in parts. In one place only, on the right, the painting was brightened by an unseen sun, where a beautiful woman in rich clothes sat at a wooden table set out in the street. There was a child with her. The light that shone on them was miraculous. In the dim hallway it seemed real, as if it were not just a trick of the paint, but had the power to illuminate.

"Sometimes, when I look at it long enough, I think I see them move."

At length Cornelia continued, "We better go get that beer."

I turned away with reluctance and found myself looking into one of the rooms that opened out of the hallway. It was bright with painted white walls and a wide bed under a white coverlet. There was a basket of flowers on the bed and I inhaled a light fragrance that enthralled me. It was Miss Widdershins' room, I was sure of it.

"Come on."

Cornelia was already at the head of the stairs.

On the way down, she told me about the painting.

"It was given to us a long time ago, in Flanders. We saved one of the painter's children from drowning, and he gave it to us in thanks. We've kept it ever since. It stays with the King. Or Queen."

The stairs to the cellar led down from the kitchen. The steps creaked under our feet. I looked around with interest, but there wasn't much in the way of cellar junk – they hadn't been living there long enough. There were a few old fashioned steamer trunks up on heavy boards to keep them off the ground. Did Miss Widdershins' basement flood? The windows were small; there wasn't much light. I saw some dim shapes covered by blankets. More trunks.

Cornelia walked over to a cylindrical plastic tub sitting on top of a board that was laid across a couple of wooden sawhorses. She held the glass under a plastic spigot and filled it up slowly.

"The Twins brew it," she explained. She held the glass up and with a loud "pouf" blew the overflow onto me. It was an interesting botanical smell that I was later to identify as hops.

"They're gonna think I was drinking it," I said.

She shrugged.

"There's plenty enough."

We had been gone a long time, but neither the man nor the woman made any comment. He only said, "Very kind of you," as he took the glass.

Miss Widdershins was absent-mindedly swirling a beautiful copper-colored liquid in a little fat-bellied glass. She was sitting with her head very close behind the man's and speaking earnestly into his ear. He was giving brief replies. I gradually became aware that I could not understand the words he was saying. I felt that our presence was an intrusion.

"*Sho ling* away!" Now Cornelia was speaking nonsense too. "Gotta go. Bye bye."

Miss Widdershins raised her glass slightly in acknowledgment. She had an intense, almost fierce expression as she conversed with her companion, an expression that I had never seen before.

3.

I followed Cornelia down the driveway to the backyard. I had no idea where we were going.

"Do you play chess?" She asked.

"A little. I know how the pieces move."

"Good enough. Do you want to play?"

"Sure."

She climbed the back stairs and led me into the house again. Now she was moving quietly. We crept down into the basement once more. There she brought out a couple of candles in Wee Willie Winkie-style candle holders, lit them and placed them on either side of one of the steamer trunks. We laid the chess board between them and played across the trunk. The pieces were actually carved and polished stone, black and white, and the board was dark wood and ivory inlay. We sat on empty plastic crates. It was great fun, I thought, but I soon became aware that Cornelia was not paying strict attention. Every once in a while she got up and walked to the front of the basement, where she stood opposite the front stoop and listened for voices. I went with her the first couple of times;

there was a crawlspace under the front porch that was open in parts to the basement, and if you stood in the right place and were quiet enough, you could hear indistinct voices.

I soon tired of the surveillance. Cornelia kept it up for a while, but she didn't hear whatever she was listening for, and she lost the first game. After that she started paying closer attention, and won the second game handily. The rubber match was a lengthy struggle. We had used up our meager stores of concentration and we both missed opportunity after opportunity.

"This is pathetic," I said at length.

"Isn't it?"

We were rescued from our incompetence when the cellar door opened and we heard someone descending the stairs.

A man was singing his way down:

Farewell ye dungeons dark and strang
Farewell farewell to thee
MacPherson's time will nae be lang
On yonder gallows tree

Cornelia rose.

The man caught sight of us as soon as his head cleared the ceiling.

"What's this?" he said. "What's this?"

"Welcome home. *Míle míle fáilte.*"

"Is that little Cornelia?"

"Yes. I wanted to be here to welcome you."

"Look how tall. When I left you were a little bit of a thing."

They embraced.

"Will you be staying here now?"

"No, no, there are people enough as it is."

"It's a big house."

"They found me another place close by. It wouldn't do for me to stay here anyway."

"I thought you were free and clear."

"Oh, surely, surely. But still, a record is a record."

He turned to me for the first time, and I got my first good look at him. He was a good deal smaller than the other men I had seen at the house, only about as tall as Cornelia. He was neater in appearance and dress than the others, and lacked their air of menace, but still I fancied I would have recognized him as one of them even if I had met him on the street instead of here in Miss Widdershins' basement. He regarded me with pale eyes that gave the impression of habitual melancholy even in the midst of this joyful homecoming.

"*Fer bullug, eh?*" I heard him say.

Cornelia teetered her head to and fro in a noncommittal gesture.

"*Sha is nee,*" I heard her say.

He raised his eyebrows and twisted his mouth into a skeptical expression, but he let her answer stand.

"There's supposed to be a bag down here, a blue bag."

Cornelia walked over and pulled a long string, and a bare bulb brightened the basement. He soon found what he was looking for, a well-stuffed duffel bag sitting atop a pile of others, all resting on the broad top of a black trunk.

He hefted it, then swung it over his shoulder.

"Stay a while," said Cornelia. "*Fan go foil.*"

"Don't worry, you'll be seeing a lot of me."

"You must have a lot of stories."

"None that bear telling, or not many. It was a dreary time. I am so tired now I can barely stand, I just want to get home and close my eyes. I promise I'll be back soon."

He gave her a pat on the head and started up the stairs.

After the door closed behind him, Cornelia turned to me.

"Well, that was a little disappointing. Still, I should be grateful we have him back. I don't think he trusts you. He thinks you're a Bellyman."

"Well, I am, aren't I?"

"I keep forgetting."

"Where was he?" I asked, but I thought I knew.

"In prison. He didn't do anything wrong, it was on weapons

charges. See he used to be our *Army Jerry*, he was the one who kept our weapons. We don't use the police, so we have to do for ourselves. In some places, like New York, they throw you in jail if they catch you with weapons. So he went to prison for all of us really."

I nodded.

"For Uncle Tom especially."

I nodded again.

"Uncle Thomas is *cooree*: the champion. He can't go to prison or he'd have to give it up."

I didn't know what to make of this. "What does the champion do?"

"He takes care of the rest of us. Especially the Dragons, especially the Queen."

"And sometimes he needs weapons?"

"Not often. Sometimes."

I thought I had probably used up my quota of questions, but she kept talking.

"Like now, we're looking for someone. One of us went off, went away, and they want him back."

"You're not allowed to leave?"

"Oh, sure, you can leave if they trust you. It's called 'leaving clean' – *glanagoil*. When you're out, you're out. Don't bring the world back in on us. But they don't trust him. I think he took something with him too, something we want, something that could make trouble for us, but they won't tell me what it is. I'm sure of it. I've been trying to find out. It's got something to do with the Geese, too, with the Regiment. Aunt Vivien doesn't want them to know he's gone or it's gone, whatever it is. She wants to get it back before they find out.'

She paused, then exhaled through pursed lips in a long breathy whistle.

"Con, Con Gone-away," she said. "I never liked him. He was more like a … not like a Dragon at all."

She looked up along the cellar stairs at the closed door.

"They won't tell me anything, but I'll find out. It's a contest.

I will pit my mighty brain against them all. Hey, do you want to help me?"

"What can I do?"

"You can be my agent. An extra set of eyes and ears."

"I don't think I know enough to be of any use. What am I looking and listening for?"

"Your ignorance is your best weapon. Who would suspect such a simpleton?"

"Thanks. But half the time I don't even know what your family is saying, when they're not talking directly to me."

"Oh, that's our lingo, *ar djanga fain*. I'll help you out."

"What is it? Where does it come from?"

"It's a mishmash. Some Gaelic with a lot else mixed in. Everywhere we've lived. There's French and a lot of English, and some Gammon and some words I don't even know where they come from. Some real old words too, I think they might be Welsh. It's a little different from group to group. With the Geese it's mainly just Gaelic, kind of old-fashioned, though."

"How do you talk to each other?"

"We get by."

"I can't possibly learn that."

"You don't need to. I'll clue you in on what you need to know. So, are you going to help me?"

"Sure, I'll do what I can."

We shook on it. What was the harm? I was fairly sure it would all lead nowhere.

5. The Estate

1.

Another long week between weekends. The end of the year was in sight now; after a late Easter it would just be a sprint to the summer. There was a lot of work to be done, though, more than I had ever seen in grammar school. They gave us projects. The worst was biology, where we had to write up something based on our experiments. I can only bring it to mind with great difficulty. They had me cutting the tails off some tadpoles. I forget why; I think the tails were supposed to grow back. I don't believe they grew back on the animals, but I'm fairly sure they grew back on the paper I submitted.

There was one non-academic event that I remember quite well. I was seated in the lunch room, the "commons" we called it. By this point, the blooming buzzing confusion of the first few months had subsided, and we freshman felt at home. Trey and I had worked out a system, whereby he saved a seat for me while I got both our lunches. We always found seats, usually with a group of our friends. It was toward the end of the week and toward the end the lunch period, and I was sitting at my ease digesting my meal. Trey had gone up for seconds, since, as he said, his muscles needed the extra fuel for recovery. I gradually became aware of a presence in Trey's seat. I turned and found myself facing the dreaded Heyward.

He smiled pleasantly.

"So, how is freshman year treating you?"

"OK," I said warily.

"Good, good. It can be a difficult adjustment. You take the Queens Bus, don't you?"

"Yeah."

"That can be difficult, too, I've heard. There have been suicides."

"It's all right."

"Fine, fine. How about biology? How's the biology project going?"

"It's due in a couple of weeks."

"That was always a tough one. Choppin' on frogs and lizards. That really separates the men from the boys."

He nodded thoughtfully.

"Choppin' on frogs."

"Yo!"

Trey had returned. He looked determined.

"You're in my chair."

"I beg your pardon."

"You're in my chair!"

"This?"

"That. You're in my chair. Get out of it."

"But if it's your chair, why am I sitting in it? See what I'm saying? I'm sitting in it, so it must be my chair."

Something about Heyward's bland smile must have infuriated Trey because he reached down and grabbed a chair leg, jerking the chair out from under his enemy. Heyward's legs were strong enough that he didn't even lose balance, just stood up.

"Oh! Little Man! Little Man is fierce!" He smiled again. "OK, you can have your chair. Have your chair and eat your, what is it, rice pudding? Damn! Eat up."

He sauntered away. It was a pointless exercise, but Trey seemed pleased with the outcome. It worried me, though. I thought Heyward must have something in mind.

2.

As it happened, I was working over some biology homework on the next Saturday morning, when I heard a sharp knock at the front door. Someone else's problem, I thought.

I heard my sister's voice outside my room.

"Estella is here."

She had worked her way through a number of nicknames for Cornelia and Miss Widdershins. "Give my regards to Miss Nipperkin and Lobelia," she would say as I left the house. At length, to her delight, she hit on Miss Havisham and Estella, and she stuck with that one. I, of course, was Pip.

I hadn't recognized Cornelia's knock; it was louder and more insistent than usual.

"Where were you?" she demanded, as soon as I opened the front door.

I was perplexed.

"I was upstairs."

She actually stamped her foot with impatience.

"I mean earlier this morning."

I must have gazed at her blankly.

"Didn't you get my note?"

"What note?"

We had a little old bronze mailbox mounted on one of the wooden posts that supported the roof over our stoop. She plunged her hand into it and drew out a square unstamped envelope.

"I left it here Tuesday night. Don't you open your mail?"

"Oh the mailman never uses that anymore. It's too small; he can't fit the catalogs in it. He just leaves our mail on the landing."

"So strange," Cornelia shook her head.

"What does it say?"

She handed it to me. It contained an assignment. Early that morning the Widdershins household was expecting a visit from their "soliciter." I was to remain concealed behind the garage or some other place suitable to the task and then follow him on his departure.

Cornelia watched me as I read. "See, I can't follow him, he knows me."

"Suppose he drives away?"

"He never does."

"Why would I follow him?"

I saw myself trailing after a stranger like a lonely kitten.

"To find out where he lives. Then we could put the place under surveillance. Everyone passes through there. Maybe we could sneak in when he's out."

I was beginning to fear that being Cornelia's agent might carry with it some peril. I recalled that it had rained hard all the previous night and most of the morning. Had she expected me to wait through the rain?

"Oh … sorry," I said.

"That's OK. Too late now. We can use this box as a secret mail drop, though. It's perfect. Just remember to check it every once in a while."

"You know I can't promise to be available all the time. Sometimes I might have to do something. Sometimes I might be away."

"I know. What are you doing now?"

"Homework. Biology homework."

"Can I see?"

"Seriously?"

We went up to my room and she gazed at the open biology textbook on my desk.

"What is all this stuff? I thought biology was about plants."

"It is supposed to be what the plants are made of. I guess this part is more chemistry, really."

She started leafing through the book, sometimes stopping to pore over the illustrations. She flipped to the back and looked at the index.

"I don't think I could do this," she said sadly.

"Well, you don't have to. Anyway, it's high school stuff."

She shut the book.

"It looks really hard," she said. "I should go."

I shrugged.

"I was going to finish it later anyway."

When we got downstairs my sister and my mother were loading a cooler with drinks and sandwiches.

"Maybe Cornelia would like to go to Westfields with us," my sister suggested. She was always glad to have Cornelia around; she found her an interesting and sympathetic character.

"Where are you going?"

"Westfield Gardens. It's out on the Island. It's an old estate with a mansion and the most beautiful flower gardens. We go there all the time; we're members. There's probably not that much growing there this early. Later in the summer is best, when the roses bloom. But it's always worth seeing. We're going on a picnic."

"Would you like to go? You could call your aunt and ask her," my mother said.

"We don't have a phone," Cornelia said.

"Really, no phone? Well ... it's a nuisance most of the time."

"I would like to go."

"Maybe we can stop on our way and ask your aunt if she wouldn't mind you going."

Cornelia nodded.

"Good idea."

I didn't think it was such a good idea. I wanted to keep our two households separate. I didn't think anything good could come from exposing my parents to the parade of ex-cons and hatchet men who passed through Miss Widdershins' front door. I was always a little nervous even when they spent too much time with Cornelia.

Nevertheless, when the time came we piled into the car and headed off towards Miss Widdershins' house. My grandfather stayed home; he wanted to sleep. It seemed he was sleeping more and more.

When we got to the house, the place was overrun with people I had never seen before. There were two pickup trucks parked, one in the driveway and one actually in the weeds of the front yard. Men were moving back and forth over the lawn and down the driveway. One man was standing in the truck in the driveway handing down building supplies. I could hear him singing a slow song in a hoarse voice. They were a rough-looking crew; I could see that they were Dragons. One of the bodyguards was standing in the front doorway, at his ease, surveying the scene with his familiar cigar in his mouth. I could tell them apart by now. This was the one who had been sitting outside the door the first time I entered Miss Widdershin's house.

My father slowed the car and Cornelia, who was seated between my sister and me, leaned across me and stuck her head out the window. I got a faceful of her springy curly hair. She gave a shrill loud whistle.

"Hey, cousin!" she shouted. "Hey, cuz! Is Aunt Vivien around?"

The bodyguard shook his head and walked over to the car.

"Hello, Cornelia. She's away. She wanted to get away from the noise; we're fixing up the shed."

"When you see her, tell her I went on a picnic with the Wards."

My father got out of the car and talked things over with the bodyguard. They were just about of a size and of similar coloring, but my father had a scholarly air about him that the other most definitely lacked. They spoke for a while. Then they shook hands and my father got back in the car.

"He says it's OK. We'll have you back by four anyway. He's your cousin?"

"Yep."

"Too bad," said my mother. "I wanted to meet your aunt."

3.

From the point of view of distance, it was not a long drive to Westfield, but the time of travel varied considerably. The route took us on the Long Island Expressway, and the traffic could always grind to a halt without warning or apparent reason. I think it was an easy trip that day.

"What is that piece?" asked my mother of no one in particular. She liked to listen to the radio in the car. "Isn't that lovely? I wonder who is the composer."

"Sounds like Scarlatti," said Cornelia.

We all looked at her with surprise, my father glancing up at the rear view mirror.

"My mother listens to that stuff all the time," Cornelia explained apologetically.

There was a brief silence, and then my sister said what we all were thinking.

"Your mother? She *listens* to it?"

"All the time."

We had all assumed that Cornelia was an orphan.

"Oh. I'm sorry, I thought ... Does your mother live with your aunt?"

"No. She's out in Pennsylvania somewhere. "

Cornelia picked up on the awkward silence.

"She moves around a lot. She sent me to live with Aunt Vivien for a while. It's something we do. It's kind of a tradition in my family. We go live with a close relative for a piece of time."

"Wow, I wouldn't like that," said my sister. "I can't imagine going to live with Aunt Joanne. I don't think I could take Troll 24/7."

Now Cornelia was surprised.

"What's Troll?"

"My cousin Eugene."

"You call him Troll?"

"He calls himself Troll. You'd have to know him."

Cornelia smirked.

"He got his car, you know," my mother said.

"Uh oh, he lives out here, too. Drive carefully."

I always liked the approach to Westfields. "Our estate," we used to call it. Once it had belonged to some coal magnate or other, but now it was open to the public.

We entered through a tall black iron gate, and then drove a long straight narrow approach, attended by a row of old high trees on either side. However often we came there, it was always a thrill. Sometimes, when there was an event like a concert or an exhibition, it was crowded and we had to drive off into a field to park, but this early in the year there were only a few people around, so we could stay in the main lot.

The big attractions of the place were the house and surrounding gardens. My mother liked to look through the house, but it bored me; I preferred wandering the grounds. As it turned out, the house wasn't open to the public yet this early in the season, so we all stayed outside. I took Cornelia on a tour. There was a lot to see: enormous old smooth-barked European beeches, a duck pond, statues of Greek gods, fragrant boxwood hedges. It was easy to get lost and I always tried to do so. There were still places I had not yet seen, for the grounds extended for great distances in many directions, and there were always new hitherto unsuspected lawns and buildings hidden behind high hedges that revealed themselves on each visit.

When we visited the flower gardens we found that there were mainly bulbs growing. Some I had never seen before. Cornelia was taken by one in particular, a little blue creation, a jonquil I think it was, with small petals. She squatted down and peered at it, studying it for a long time like a patron in an art gallery. I liked the air there, mellowed by the scent of non-fragrant growing things.

We spent a long time up and down the garden paths, walking under bare trellises and through gaps in brick walls. Most of the time we were alone.

"Could you imagine living here?" said Cornelia.

"I usually do," I said. "But you'd need a small army of people to take care of the place."

"We could do it," said Cornelia, and I knew she meant the Dragons.

At last we turned back from the gardens. Approached from the rear, the house stood atop a plateau, reachable by two sets of stairs cut into the retaining wall, one on the left and one on the right. It dominated the plain below like a Rhineland castle. We took the separate stairs, then came together at the top, and leaned over the railing looking down.

"I am going to remember this place," said Cornelia. "I am going to remember this day."

When we got back to the others they had already begun the business of spreading out the picnic. We sat at a wooden picnic table, and there was a humorous fuss made of avoiding the inevitable bird droppings. We weren't big eaters in my family, so we finished fairly quickly. I had a momentary fear that Cornelia would ask my father for beer, but she was content with soda. She had learned that much of our strange customs.

My family spread out some blankets and sat in the grass. I would have been just as happy to sit down with them, but Cornelia was soon off again, tearing away like an Irish setter, racing the length of a long expanse of grass while I trotted along behind her. When we reached the end and turned around, we got a clear view back to the big house where it shone in the sun, red brick walls and a steep dark roof broken up by chimneys and gabled windows. It seemed as if it was a mile away, though I don't suppose it was so far. The green lawn unrolled from the house to our feet like a living carpet. I could see my family sitting under the trees halfway between us and the house. We had come to the end of the estate.

Cornelia broke the silence at length.

"I smell horses," she said.

She went wandering back in the general direction of the house, but off to the right among some tall widely spaced trees. Sure enough, it wasn't long before she found her horses in a field behind white rail fences. I didn't know if they were part of the estate, or if we had come to the first neighbors.

Cornelia sat comfortably on the fence and watched the horses. There were only two of them, two smooth brushed chestnuts.

"I used to ride a lot when I was with my mother. We lived in the country most of the time. There was always somewhere to ride."

"Did you own horses?"

"We didn't, but somebody always did. I miss horses. They're better than bicycles."

Then she said, "I wonder if they'd let me ride them."

She ran through a repertoire of clucking noises. The horses ignored her. They had neither saddle nor bridle so I was relieved that they didn't come over, since I could easily see her talking me up on one of them. Cornelia slipped off the fence and walked toward them. When she got close they turned their backs to her and trotted lightly away. She gave up and came back.

"I don't suppose we'll do the ride this year, not in the city."

She explained: "Every year we go night riding, twice a year. You have to be old enough. I went for the first time last year. It's great fun. We should be going soon, on May Eve. I bet they'll go in Pennsylvania."

"What do you do?"

"We go riding at night. It's best under a moon. We just tear around and cause trouble. It's hard to describe. There's really nowhere to do it in the city."

I considered.

"How about down by the water? Along the beach."

"It's possible. But there are too many police around now. Aunt Vivien said that it's worse than ever, there are police everywhere. Soldiers, too."

"Does your aunt go on the ride?"

"Are you kidding? She leads it. You should see her up there seated on a good horse, all in red with the moon on her hair. She's a good rider. They say that's when Uncle Tom first saw her, on the November ride."

"Does the Regiment do the night ride?"

"Nah, they're too serious. They just drink and tell war stories." She laughed.

I remembered my family.

"We'd better go back," I said.

The family was packed and ready to go when we reached them. We trudged back to the car; we were all sleepy from a day spent in the fresh air. We arranged ourselves in the back as before. As soon as we left Westfield and picked up speed along the main road, Cornelia fell asleep like a child. She tipped her curly head onto my shoulder and sank into comfortable oblivion. I rode home with her curls pressed against my cheek and ear. I could see that my mother thought we were cute, which was offensive, but there was nothing I could do about it.

4.

We all spoke softly on the way home. For a long while, my father whistled in a meditative fashion, and broke it off just as we pulled off the highway onto the service road.

"*Come by the Hills*," he said. "I think that's the tune that fella was singing, the one standing on the truck."

My father whistled it again to demonstrate.

"So you both named that tune," said my mother, for the man on the radio had confirmed Cornelia's guess as well.

"He always sings that." Cornelia spoke from my shoulder. "We call it *Buachaill ón Éirne*. It's an old tune. It's got a lot of names."

"Did you have a good sleep, dear?"

"Yes, thanks."

Cornelia still had not straightened up.

"What did you call it?" my father asked, looking in the mirror with a curious expression.

"*Buachaill ón Éirne*. It's about some guy from Loch Erne, I think. Over in Ireland. It's an old tune. A very good tune."

Cornelia yawned.

"Where are we?"

"Just turning past the church."

She raised her head and looked around.

"Boy, I was tired. Aunt Vivien says I don't eat enough."

"It's the fresh air," suggested my mother.

"I doubt it," said Cornelia, yawning again. "I'm always outside. Uncle Tom says I'm feral."

We rolled up to her house.

The trucks and the workmen were gone. The two bodyguards were standing on either side of the newly trimmed lawn. They had between them a great twisted piece of wood, a stump that had been wrested out of the earth with the cut remains of roots springing in all directions, and they were amusing themselves by tossing it back and forth, cursing when they were scored by the projecting spikes.

Cornelia rose in her seat and leaned over into the front of the car. She threw her arms around my mother's neck and kissed her on the cheek.

"Thank you for inviting me, Mrs. Ward, I had a lovely time."

The bodyguards had stopped their game and were looking at us.

"Bye." Cornelia wriggled past me, and bounced out into the street and up onto the lawn.

One of the men stepped up and held the door open for her; she stopped in the doorway and gave us a final wave.

"Well, that was a nice afternoon," my mother said. "She's a sweet child."

"With an extensive background in musical appreciation," my father added. "I'm strangely tired too. That place must have cast a spell on us."

"So who are those guys?" said my sister in a voice pitched only for the back seat.

"Cornelia's cousins, apparently."

"Do they all live together? I see them all at church every Sunday."

"I don't think so. Actually, I don't know. They might. They're usually around, especially the one we saw this morning."

"What's his name?"

"Balin. I don't know his last name."

"Balin? What's his brother's name? No, don't tell me, don't tell me … Dwalin."

"Actually, it's Balan."

"His brother's name is Balin too?" My sister burst out laughing. "This is my brother Balin. This is my other brother Balin."

"No, Balan, with an 'a.' Not Balin, with an 'i.' " But I had to laugh too; and my sister forgot to ask any more questions.

6. The Explanation

My mother again had hopes of speaking to Miss Widdershins that Sunday, but she was forestalled by the crowd. People always showed up in droves for the palms. They were monetarily worthless, but, as my sister said, people always like to get something for nothing. My grandfather said that churches used to be filled like that every Sunday. He stayed home; he avoided anything that had to do with a crowd in those days. He always needed to be able to get quickly to the exits.

There was a big die-off among the tadpoles that week. I marked it in my diary. "Weird Shadow over Innsmouth," I wrote. I had been reading about those semi-batrachian coast dwellers in H.P. Lovecraft's story, and I made a mental connection with our biology frogs. The shadow was the sudden passing of the hand of death over almost all of them. They turned blue, floated upside down, and stank up the refrigerator. It was a grim odor indeed, not easily forgotten, too easily recalled, even now. No one knew what had happened, but we all had our data by then, so I suppose they were expendable. I don't know how they felt about the whole odd affair, but I don't imagine they were pleased.

The week was spent in anticipation of the Easter Vacation. We started the subjunctive in Latin, which was something of a thrill. I remember Latin in those early days when the paradigms were laid out perfectly clearly in tables, and every sentence followed a predictable structure. More like a puzzle than a language. Later on came the stylists, Caesar and Catullus, Cicero and finally Virgil, and we found that we had only just started the first steps down the road. But now it was simple progressions, a discrete new topic each week, one week to the next, one lesson to the next.

I discovered a letter from Cornelia on Thursday, in our secret drop box. It was sort of an un-invitation. It was drawn in thick bright blue ink across textured off-white stationary, with a lot of corrections and thorough cross outs of errors. She must have used a fountain pen.

Dear James,   *April 17, Holy Thursday*
                               Commonly St. Donan's Day

Let me wish you a Happy Easter. I hope to see you at Mass and present compliments of the season in person.

We are expecting a full house of visitors on Easter. Some of my close kinfolk will be there, and even some of the Regiment who are stationed in the area. We expect to receive Mac Owen's son, and we will all do our best to make him welcome.

This week has been and will continue to be a busy one, so I don't expect that we will be able to make our usual Saturday rendezvous. It might also be best not to perplex our visitors by the presence of a Bellyman in the bosom of our family. I hope this does not sound ungracious. You know you are always welcome to us.

By good fortune all the next week you will be free, and we can go visiting throughout the week. Please come and see me.

Thank you again for taking me to see your family's estate. It is just the kind of place I would like to live, only I would of course like to be nearer the sea.

Your devoted friend,

Cornelia Parsons

I hadn't been expecting to see Cornelia over the Easter weekend. We had our own family obligations to attend to, which usually involved some cooking and a lot of driving.

We generally attended all the services of the Easter Triduum.

I always liked the rhythm of it, including the long pause on Easter Saturday, which seemed like the quietest day of the year. It was an awful lot of time to spend in church for the likes of me, and I wasn't crazy about some of the liturgies – I never liked the reenacted washing of the feet which seemed to me to flirt with farce – but it all fit together pretty well. The whole was greater than the sum of the parts. I didn't see the Widdershins Group on Easter, but I did see them on Good Friday sitting near the front, with Miss Widdershin's yellow hair shrouded by a black veil, and Cornelia looking thin in a black dress, and the bodyguards looking as they always looked.

We took our vacation the week after Easter, whereas the public schools had already had their spring break. That sometimes made family visits hard to coordinate, since most of my cousins went to public school. I had won a full scholarship to my high school; that was how we could afford the tuition. It was a prestigious school, and I always felt a little guilty about the scholarship. It was given, I am sure, in the expectation that the eager recipient would use it as the first step in an ascent to academic or financial prominence, a climb where one achievement built on another, stretching beyond college to a successful, respected, even honored middle age. It was clear to me that I would never amount to anything, and it seemed a pity to waste their money for them. I was surprised no one else saw it. It must have been the grades that fooled them.

2.

I wandered over to Miss Widdershins' house mid-week on a sunny morning. When I arrived I found Miss Widdershins herself kneeling in the driveway, working the fresh dirt by the side of the house. All the bushes, weeds and vines had been cleared away by the work crew the previous week, and the beginnings of a garden were taking shape in their place. When Miss Widdershins saw me she called me over.

"Wait for a minute here," she said, "I want to talk to you."

I stood and watched her work. Her hands moved decisively,

using a trowel to scoop out neat portions of dirt and replace them with precut plugs, each with a sprout already growing through the center. She wore a sleeveless sack dress despite the chill, and knelt on a pad. I watched her round bare arms as she worked, lost in admiration. She was a strong woman; when she worked the trowel in the ground I could see the soft muscles in her forearms swelling and shifting under her smooth skin. From shoulder to glove her arms were bare, scratched red in a few places. She braced on her left arm and worked with her right and I was fascinated by the complex of shapes, all working in concert. It was like a statue come to life, I thought. She really had the most extraordinary arms. They were pre-industrial arms, I said to myself, not even sure what I meant by the phrase.

After not too long, she stopped working, sat back on her haunches, straightened, and wiped her brow with the back of her hand.

"That will do for a while."

She stood up, peeled off her gardening gloves, and dropped them in the driveway. Someone else would clear it all away.

When she faced me, I saw a streak of dirt across her forehead where she had wiped her hand and a light glow of sweat on her face. I was always a little nervous when I was alone with her, never sure of my eyes. Even now, the shapeless design of the dress only served to draw attention to the shape of the woman wearing it. I felt that I was sweating myself.

"Cornelia's away at the moment, but she is expected back shortly. Come inside, this is a good opportunity for us to talk things over. There are things you should understand."

She led me into the house.

"Sit. I'll be back in a moment."

I sat in my chair, the same chair I'd sat in when I first entered the house and Cornelia made the tea for us. I listened to a new pendulum clock ticking on the wall. I looked around for other novelties, and saw a small bookcase by the stairs. Many of the books had pale cream covers, a material I was much later to identify as vellum, and the spines were handwritten. I was debating whether I should slide one of them out and take a look at it, when Miss Widdershins returned. She was wearing her snug blue jacket over an indoor dress and looked like she had freshly washed in cold water. There were wet strands of hair framing her face.

She sat in her familiar position on the couch.

"I have wanted to have a nice sit-down chat with you for some time, but we have both been so busy. There are many things that ought to be explained to you. I am sure Cornelia has told you something about us, yes?"

"Yes, a little."

"But only a little. She has a lively mind, but unsystematic. What did she tell you?"

"She said that you all came from over the sea a long time ago. She said that you are sort of a tribe and you keep to yourselves. She said that you are the Queen."

"All true enough, as far as it goes. Anything else?"

"She says that you have your own language. A mixture of Gaelic and a lot of other things."

"A lot of other things. Again, true enough. Anything else?"

"She said that there are different groups. Dragons, Cats. The Regiment."

"Good. That's a place to start."

She closed her eyes and took a few slow breaths.

"We came, all of us, at various times, from the islands north of France and Spain. When things got difficult in our homelands we moved to the continent. We have been drifters, nomads, for a long time, although I believe that we have served our adopted lands well when we have been able. You have heard of the Wild Geese, for an example?"

I nodded.

"After Limerick, after the Treaty of Limerick, they moved in their thousands to France. For a while they served the King over the Water. Then as the hope of return faded they served the French King only. Then the Revolution came and he too was lost, and they had to find other accommodations. Most simply settled in their new homes and adapted to the new order as best they could.

Some tried to restore the French king, but most of those were led by guile down other paths, to die on tropic shores. But some … they became the Regiment, or the Geese as we call them. As the Brigades closed down in Europe – in France, Spain, the Empire, Italy – they became a new nation without borders, a secret nation with their own elected colonel as their ruler. For most, soldiering was all they knew, and they became the eternal soldiers, swords in the service of nations that did not know them. It was not … it is not uncommon for them to fight on opposite sides of the same conflict. Many came, as all nations do, to the New World."

"We the Dragons left earlier. When the ship left Loch Swilly in 1608 with the royalty of Ulster on board – the Flight of the Earls you may have heard about – there were some of us who sailed with her. In fact, by that time there were already a lot of us on the continent. We were exiles of long standing."

She paused suddenly and collected herself, bowing her head and placing the inside of her wrist against her forehead.

"Och, I'm worse than Cornelia," she said. "I am being needlessly cryptic. Let me begin again. Listen. We – my family, my tribe, my nation – we are the Dragons. We have had that name from long ago. Britain was once our home. We were a royal race. In the general ruin of the world that came with the fall of Rome, Britain was not spared. It's a story that has often been told. A sad and a foolish story. The Britons fought one another like jackals, although there were no spoils to the victor. A kingdom divided cannot stand. When the strangers came in strength and in numbers, we left for the lands of the Gael where we lived for a thousand years, one little kingdom among many. When the world changed again, a second ruin of Rome, we emigrated to the mainland, and to the New World after that. That was the Second Exile. You will not read about it in history books. The others, the Geese and the Cats and the rest, they only became exiles at this time, in the destruction of the Gael, in the seventeenth century and afterward. For them this was the first exile, do you understand? The Geese I told you about; the Cats were from Scotland mainly. Most of them left to follow their king. The particulars don't matter now. As the elder brothers, so to speak, the Dragons have always been given primacy in honor. My father was the King of the Dragons, so he was the first man among all the tribes. As his only surviving child, I am the Queen."

She peered at me.

"Is any of this making sense to you?"

"Oh, yeah, sure, I think so," I said, resolving to spend some time with the books as soon as I got home.

"The history is perhaps of secondary importance. Maybe it no longer matters. There are many … nuances. A hundred stories of a hundred families all woven together. Some of it is as simple as like calling to like. The important thing to understand is that this, this thing of ours, *Ár Rud* we call it, is our secret. *Ár Rud ár rún*, as we say. No one outside the tribes knows the tribes."

"That's not to say they're all like us. We all take different approaches to the problem. The Regiment are out in the world. For most of the time, you'd never know they were any different from the rest of you. They have all the proper numbers that one must have to exist in your world. Their papers are in order. Most go to the same schools alongside you. They serve in your military. They simply live by a different law, a secret supreme law that takes precedence over every other law. They 'follow the drum,' as they say. We Dragons do it a little differently. We try to leave no footprint, or as little as possible. We wish to pass among you as ghosts. This is true in particular of the royal household. You can appreciate that this is becoming more difficult with each passing day. Your people track everything. The simple act of buying a house …"

Her voice trailed off. She seemed to forget about me for a while, then quietly she began again.

"That Cats are a little of this and a little of that. They make it up as they go along; they're like Tinkers. I admire their insouciance. They're the fewest in number but they may be the safest."

"Under these circumstances, you can see that our … our invisibility is vital to our survival. We wish to respect your laws, but it's really impossible. We break a dozen laws a day without thinking. Every time money changes hands, work is performed, food and drink are served, game is collected, animals are raised. Our nurturing of our own children is an offense. Our administration of justice, our enforcement of judgements, is an outrage."

"These are just the legal aspects of the dilemma. In truth, the social dilemma is the more intractable. No state would tolerate a society such as ours, a little self-enclosed kingdom, whose ideas are so different, whose visions are so strange, living within it. They would kidnap our children, shatter our households, dishonor our memories, rape our privacy.

"But these are things that I think you know already, or can guess. I've kept you long enough and Cornelia is at the door. I thank you for your patience. Thus endeth lesson the first," she said with a smile.

3.

Cornelia was standing in the doorway. She looked surprised.

"Hello, James," she said. Then she dipped a shoulder and swung a pack off her back. "Here, Aunt Vivien. It's all here, he says."

She brought the pack over to the sofa and pulled out a thick accordion folder, tied up with string.

"Thank you, Cornelia. O, sweetie, this is so heavy, I had no idea."

"*De rien.* Is James free?"

"As you see him."

"I mean, are you finished with him?"

"I have finished telling him what I wished to tell him."

"C'm'ere." Cornelia made a motion to the door with her head. I could see she was excited about something.

I rose.

"Poor James," said Miss Widdershins. "Surrounded by such imperious women. Such is too often the fate of a gentleman."

"Nonsense." That was Cornelia, not me. I just smiled with vague benevolence and followed her out.

As soon as we got outside, Cornelia began speaking rapidly

in a low voice.

"I was at the solicitor's house. Not the one I wanted you to follow but the other one. See, we have two main lawyers, one for our own law, and one to help us deal with you guys. *Sean Nós* and *Nós Nua,* Old Style and New Style, or as I call them, Big Nose and Little Nose, for a different reason."

"Whose house were you at today?"

"*Sean Nós,* Old Style. That's the one with the big nose. He's a little guy with a big nose, like a wise old secretary bird, and he knows absolutely everything. He can recite the trees going back a hundred generations. He knows all the histories, all the judgements. All the current branches, too. I don't know how he remembers it all."

"So your aunt sent you there?"

"I don't know what they were thinking. Aunt Vivien wanted me to pick up some papers about the Geese. I sat in his parlor while he collected them. He has a bunch of tall cabinets with pigeonholes all crammed with rolled-up papers. He was mumbling to himself the whole time he looked through them. He's really nice. I like him a lot even if he does still think I'm eight years old."

I saw nothing here to explain Cornelia's excitement. I must have looked perplexed.

"Two things," she said, holding up the appropriate number of fingers. "One: I know where he lives now. It's in easy striking distance. It's as good as knowing whether the other one lives. Better maybe. Anything we want to know is there if I can find it."

She paused, "Two: I know what Con Gone-away took."

We were sitting now on the front steps, and before Cornelia continued, she stood up and peered into the porch to make sure no one was listening. She sat back down right next to me, hip to hip, and looked into my eyes.

"He took the Lion, the *Black Book of Leuven.*"

She saw that this did not make an impression on me.

"It's a big book, a really huge black book that the Dragons made years ago. They were living in a city in French Flanders called Leuven – or Louvain the French call it – when they put it together. It's really a bunch of different books all bound together in one. They used to do that with books. It's all sorts of different things together, all stuff they wanted to save from the old country. Some of it was copied out new, but some of it is really old. One section of it is even shorter than the others; they just tied it in with the rest."

"Why did he take it?"

"Just meanness, I guess. I don't think it would be worth much to anyone but us. The biggest section is our history, the Dragon's history from the beginning. It's unfinished, they've just kept adding to it over the years. All these columns and columns of tiny words in black ink. You should see the letters, all the points and curves packed close together, like a thorn bush. See, it's history, but it's also the law. The Dragons used to consult it a lot as a law book. That's why Aunt Vivien wants it so much now. I think it would prove her case, prove she's got the sovereignty, so that even MacOwen would have to see it."

"Didn't they make any copies?"

"Parts of it. But copies are never as good as the original, legally speaking. So now we know. We know what he took. Next thing is, we have to find out where he went. I bet he's in the city. That's why there are so many of us here. Not just the court, but the hunters too. They're looking."

"What'll they do when they find him?"

"Well, they'll get the book back for one, and anything else he took."

"What will they do with him?"

"Ça depend. So, what was Aunt Vivien talking to you about?"

"She was talking about the Dragons and the rest. All about their history."

"All about? Not by a long shot, believe me. That would take a hundred years in the telling."

Cornelia sat up straight and stretched her long arms over her head.

"Boy, I'm pooped. That pack was really heavy." She slumped back on the steps. "Entertain me. Tell me a story."

"I don't think I know any stories."

"Everybody knows stories."

I rapidly ran through possibilities in my head. *The Bremen Town Musicians?* The plot of a *Rockford* episode? *Julius Caesar,* which we were studying in English class? I remembered some of the speeches.

"Tell me about school. What's going on with that friend of yours?"

So I gave her the full story of Wilson and his enemies, up to Heyward's latest enigmatic appearance at lunch.

"I feel sure he will strike soon."

Cornelia nodded.

"God defend the right," she said.

We sat for a while more, Cornelia lounging and looking at the sky. She was still pressed hip to hip against me. I thought it would be rude to move. All at once she sat up.

"Do you hear that?"

4.

Her hearing proved better than mine. I followed her to the backyard. We found there an open air gym. One of the twins was standing at the end of the yard, near the neighbor's garage. I usually could tell them apart; I couldn't today because he was in rapid motion. He was swinging, in some programmatic way, what looked to me like a cannonball with a handle attached. (This was before kettlebells became the latest fitness fad.) Closer to us was Cornelia's Uncle Tom, engaged in an even more remarkable practice. Drawn on the ground in chalk was an elaborate circle, marked with diameters and chords and crossing lines, so that it almost looked like a sorcerer's pentangle. Cornelia's Uncle was solemnly walking the perimeter, occasionally backing up, then moving forward again, sometimes taking a step inside, always with his right arm extended straight, pointing toward the center.

The Twin began to speak to him.

"That Spanish stuff doesn't confuse you?"

"I don't get confused."

"It's too much."

The cannonball kept swinging. The Twin spoke again.

"Dancing man! Dancing man, you make me laugh."

"You're disturbing my serenity."

"Dancing man!"

"Swing your suitcase and keep quiet, you traveling salesman."

"Strong like Russian! Strong like Russian!" said the other, evidently defending his exercise of choice.

"*Éist do bheal!*"

"*Éist! Éist!*"

Their mutual abuse passed into the incomprehensible.

I saw Miss Widdershins, in her blue jacket, with a crystal drink in her hand, leaning over the railing of the back steps and surveying her menfolk with evident pride. Looking back now, I think she had a drink in her hand a lot of the time. It was like being in an episode of *Upstairs Downstairs*, or one of those other BBC serials, with a tray in every room.

Cornelia joined her on the steps, and I followed along, feeling a little uncomfortable. The two men took no notice of us. I learned later that this was a regular practice with them during the day. It brought to mind a phrase I remember from *Seinfeld*; they transformed the yard into a "fitness museum." It seemed to work for them.

Cornelia and I spent a good deal of the break visiting one another. It was my first opportunity to spend any time at Miss Widdershins' house during the week. I even discovered new members of the household – or of "the court." There was a small round woman who seemed to function as a nursemaid of some sort. She fussed over Cornelia a good deal, and also over Miss Widdershins in almost exactly the same way. Her name was Dolores. I think she must have lived at the house, though I had never seen her before.

Cornelia purchased some maps, including a large-scale map of our area of Queens, and she spent time carefully marking them with the locations of the Dragons' and associated clans' various dwellings and hangouts. She did this at my house, since it would not have been approved by the others. She kept at it over the weeks and months, frequently correcting her notations because she rarely remembered the correct names and numbers of streets on the first try. She wrote in ink. After a while, I think the notations would have been quite impenetrable to a stranger.

It was a pleasant interlude, filled with ping pong and gardening and card games. Toward the end of the week the outside world began to intrude with greater and greater insistence. My biology project was due at the end of April, the first Tuesday after we returned, and I spent most of the last weekend up in my room as I ground out the sentences hour by hour. I was dreading my return to school as a return to the crushing routine of the Monday-to-Friday emptying of time. As it so often happens, my fears were misplaced. The week to come was anything but routine. Heyward at last made his move.

7. The Ride

1.

Our Biology class met twice a week, Tuesdays and Thursdays, first period after lunch. That first Tuesday back from Easter vacation, I was in the locker room with my locker door open, in the very act of retrieving my paper for biology class, when I heard Trey swearing in the next aisle. This was no ordinary outburst. I heard him slam the locker and storm out. I had the presence of mind to return my own books and snap my padlock shut before going to investigate. Trey's locker door was still swinging open. When I looked inside I saw why he had not bothered to close it again. I was confronted by the smooth face of a brick wall. The locker had been entirely filled with bricks, cunningly fitted together so that they presented a tight and impenetrable obstacle. They were not mortared it turned out, but at first glance it appeared that they might well have been. It was a nifty piece of work; when the authorities finally cleared it away they actually had to break some of the bricks up in order to get a purchase to pull out the others. I learned much later that Heyward's father was a bricklayer, which certainly helped narrow the field of suspicion. Of texts, notebooks, school supplies, and most importantly, of the biology term paper, there was no trace.

By the time I got out of the locker room and out onto the lunch room floor, Trey had located Heyward. They were surrounded by a swiftly growing crowd of happy onlookers. Trey was practically incoherent. Heyward regarded him with an air of avuncular concern.

"Where is it? Where is it?"

"Slow down, young fellow. You seem perturbed. Where is what?"

"Where is my biology paper?"

"Your biology paper? I have no interest in your biology paper."

Trey advanced on him.

"I know you took it, you ironhead dumbass. Where is it?"

It might have been the spectators, it might have been Trey's proximity or his peculiar insult, but all at once, Heyward tired of the game. He leaned in on Trey, all pretence at last dropped, and spoke directly in his face.

"Did I tell you?" he snarled. "Did I tell you? I told you. Did I tell you?"

Trey was on him, fists flying, too fast to block. He connected with Heyward's face, and again. For a brief moment the impossible became real, and it seemed that Trey's fury might carry the day as Heyward gave ground. But it was only a tactical retreat, a step back to make room. Heyward ducked down and seized Trey around the waist, then rose up and tossed him head over heels among the tangle of lunchroom chairs. Trey practically bounced up and was at him again, but Heyward again ducked down, lower, shooting for his legs. There was no flourish this time, only a simple businesslike takedown, bringing Trey to the dusty bare floor, with Heyward above him maneuvering for position. Trey kept firing with both hands from his back, but he was clearly in trouble now.

I had edged close to the fight ready to try to pull Heyward off if things got too lopsided. I found myself jostling and shoving for position and suddenly became heavily engaged with an adversary who turned out to be none other than Tucci. He must have been moving in to get closer to the action as well. When he saw who was contending with him he became enraged and grabbed hold of my collar. Wrestling with me was like wrestling with Gollum; I was quick and elusive. I ducked under his arm and moved around him to the side, wrapping my arm around his neck and trying to get behind him for my customary chokehold. We whirled round and round, adding to the general pandemonium.

I was punched in the head. Positioned as we were, it couldn't have been Tucci who hit me. Someone must have just reached in for a free poke. I never found out who it was, nor did I care much. I could tell that Tucci had no special skills, and as long as I remained at close quarters he was no danger to me.

Already the fight was over. The authorities had arrived, led by Mr. Macklin, the tall sinister assistant dean. He seized Heyward and lifted him to his feet. The other teachers, aided by some upper-classmen, left the powerful Heyward to Macklin and secured the remaining three combatants. When the initial demands for an explanation went unanswered, we were taken away and questioned separately. I sat across the table from Macklin, and played dumb, stuttering meaningless and noncommittal answers. Honor forbade cooperation, but it was an inept performance. Only Trey, as the wronged party, had the option of disclosure. Heyward, could of course make a confession if he were so minded, but no one expected that.

Macklin was joined by the dean himself, Mr. di Foglio, a smooth operator, bearded, redolent of pipe tobacco, a teacher of Greek and Latin in a former life. No one broke, but he was deep, and I believe he pieced the story together, or enough of the story to make a judgement. There was, thank goodness, no nonsense at my school about "zero tolerance."' It was an old school, and boys had been fighting there, on and off, since the nineteenth century. No one was so foolish as to expect that to stop.

There were no suspensions. I believe that they were so relieved to find that they were not dealing with a race riot, that they went easier on us than they might have. Still the sentence for me was a hard blow: Saturday detention for the month of May, which by a cruel trick of the calendar, involved five Saturdays instead of the usual four. Quite apart from the question of how I was to get to school without benefit of the school bus, it meant a whole month's missed afternoons with Cornelia. I was annoyed too, that Heyward's punishment was no worse than ours, unless there was some additional secret penalty we never heard about.

When I saw myself in the mirror, I saw bruises on my face that I did not remember receiving. That was all to the good, cheap glory, receiving the marks of the combatant without enduring the pains. Tucci cast some unkind aspersions, due to my clutching, wriggling style of wrestling, and my preference for the rear choke, but that didn't matter. I had given him a surprise, as I always did, and we both knew he would not bother me again.

I never found out what became of Trey's biology project. When I asked him, he would only say, "Don't worry about it, it's being taken care of." I hoped he had a copy on his computer, although the drawings would have to be done again.

When I got home I disclosed my bruises to my parents and explained the situation. My mother showed concern; my father interest. They regarded it as a misfortune rather than a crime, since they knew I was not a troublemaker. The real issue was the Saturday detention.

"I can drive you in," said my father. "But I'm afraid you're on your own on the way home. You can take the A train to 42nd street and then transfer to get to Penn Station. The bus is a pain, you'd have to transfer in West Farms or something."

"I don't like that," said my mother.

"Listen, just be glad Giuliani pacified the city. In the old days if they caught him wandering around down there they'd sell him for parts."

I penned a letter to Cornelia explaining that I would be missing our Saturday rendezvous. I don't think I exaggerated my part in the fracas, although I may have tried to give the impression that I was minimizing my role out of modesty. I left it in our drop-box, wondering when I would next see her.

2.

It was the night after the celebrated brawl, when I awoke to a knock at the window. I lay in the dark, trying to collect my wits. The knock was repeated, low, patient, persistent. I arose, stumbled to the window and snapped open the shade. Through the glass I saw dimly the familiar outline of Cornelia. She had somehow ascended to the tile roof that ran beneath the second story windows, and was perched immediately outside. I raised the window, as quietly as I could.

"It's May Day," she said. "Come on out. We're doing the Ride."

I was tired, I had a long week still ahead of me, and I was already in trouble, but I could smell the night breeze through the screen.

When I got outside, I found it was heavy going across the tiles. My sneakers kept slipping and I had to spread myself flat, relying on the friction of my body to keep me from sliding to earth. I inched sideways across the roof until I came to the metal awning above our back steps. I was able to lower myself from that, and joined the others waiting in the back yard.

The yard was brilliantly illuminated. There was no moon, but our neighbors, like almost everyone else, had anti-crime lights that sprang to life whenever motion was detected within their radius of concern. Cornelia waited near our garage, as far away from the light as she could get, along with two others.

"These are the Dunleavys: Aoife and Martin."

They were shy and quick and slender, and smiled at me from behind their freckles without saying a word. I'd say they were a couple of years younger than Cornelia.

"Here, put this on."

Cornelia gave me what appeared to be a helmet or a mask, produced from a small pack she was carrying. I nudged it onto my head. It smelled old and furry, but not unpleasant, and there were eyeholes through which I could see reasonably well. I found myself looking at the long face of a fox. Cornelia. The others were a hare and a whiskered wide-eyed cat.

"What am I?"

"A badger."

They all laughed.

"Let's go," said Cornelia.

And so we went. We traveled through backyards, and over fences, and sometimes across garage roofs. When we came to the open streets, we waited, then dashed across to bury ourselves in shadow on the other side. Again and again, our passage was lit by the unwelcome security lights, brighter than any moon, the sleepless demented eyes of semi-urban paranoia. When we found a gate shut, we opened it, and when we chanced upon an open gate we left it locked. When a garden hose was wrapped tight we unspooled it, when it was already loose we tied many knots. Where the garbage was out by the curb we brought it back in, and when the empty cans were already by the side of the house we cast them into the street. We lined up the recycling cans and bottles all along the sidewalk. We switched the positions of potted plants. Once or twice we stood in the back yard and howled the occupants of the house awake.

We crossed the main boulevard at a quiet place, then crept back southwards towards the businesses. We stood behind a bar and pounded on the green lid of a hollow dumpster and screamed and called until a man emerged and cursed us, and then we fled into the night. I didn't know how late it was. I thought it was well after midnight.

After we ran away from the bar we found ourselves near the park. We stopped behind my old school, where the Dunleavys pulled out fat pieces of chalk like cakes of soap, and drew on the bricks, drew quickly with accurate sweeping strokes, the figure of a stag and hunters in pursuit with dogs, like a cave painting. We walked into the deeper darkness beneath the trees, into the park, and Martin took out a whistle and played an air while the girls linked arms and took up a piping song.

Samhradh Samhradh bainne na ngamhna
Thugamar féin an Samhradh linn

When we reached the top of the rise overlooking the pond we fell silent and paused. There was a car parked in the dead end road alongside the pond, and it caught Cornelia's eye. She motioned us to silence and stole down the hill. We had removed our masks some time before; I think we were all tired of breathing their old stale air. Cornelia slipped hers back on and we all followed suit. It took us a while to maneuver into position, surrounding the car at the four points of the compass. There were people inside, locked, I suppose, in an amorous embrace. I heard low indistinct voices. We rose as one and pressed our furry faces to the windows and raised an unearthly shriek all around them. Then we fled laughing back up the hill. I heard a car door open, and a man cursing at us as if he were trying to impress someone.

At the top of the hill Cornelia bent double laughing. I looked down at the pond and up at the dark trees against the stars. This was a good night, I thought.

"Oh, you idiots!" said Cornelia.

The Dunleavys had dropped a lit book of matches in one of the park's green steel rubbish baskets. I don't know what was in it but it went up like a Christmas tree. The Dunleavys joined hands and began to dance around the blaze.

A car we had not noticed, a car rolling slowly along the road below us, suddenly stopped short. The lights above the roof switched on and began to flash and turn, red and blue.

"Cops!" said Cornelia.

The car turned and raced up the slope. It simply bumped over the curb and came right at us, straight across the open grass. I was somehow shocked by this, and shocked by how quickly it closed distance. We scattered, Cornelia and I together and the Dunleavys I know not where, howling with glee. I was grateful for their noise; Cornelia and I ran silent. I knew the Dunleavys would not be caught. I never saw them again. For all I knew they took to the air and flew away, or disappeared into the ground.

I was not so sure of myself and Cornelia. We grabbed each other by the hand, which didn't help us run any faster, but we managed to pull together and head off in an agreed direction. Off to the right, the east, was the bluff overlooking the parkway and the bay, where we had gone walking the other day. It seemed futile to get trapped against the water, although from the sound of their voices, that was where the Dunleavys had gone. Cornelia and I headed straight north, and soon found ourselves among trees and bushes where the police car could not follow. We must have made a lot of noise, though, pushing and crackling through the underbrush.

From deep cover we heard the police car rolling down a parallel path, and saw its searchlight sweeping to the east. Another car joined the hunt. We were pinned between them but neither one of them seemed to know where we were, and I knew this section of the park well. There were foot paths, and crawl paths as well, that most other people did not know. At first, I wondered why there was such a fuss about a couple of kids running around the park, and I thought the police must have been bored on a quiet night. It wasn't long, though, before I heard the siren of a fire engine in the distance and surmised that the garbage can fire must have spread.

Lying in the dark, I could almost believe it was one of my dreams. I heard voices calling out to us and stranger, remorseless-sounding, demon voices crackling over the radio. Sometimes they were very close, and it seemed we must be caught. Always the choice was before us, stay still or move, stay still or move, and the wrong choice would finish us. I desperately did not want to be caught and marched in front of parents at 2 o'clock in the morning, and perhaps endure a great deal worse. I knew that most people would not find arson amusing.

When we reached the edge of the wooded area, it seemed all the action was behind us, and we dared to run crouching, on all fours sometimes, across the park, across the very field that my grandfather and I had circled almost two months before, toward the outer limits to the North. I felt that if we could leave the park without being seen we would be safe. Our luck did not hold. Just as we approached the limit of the park, I heard Cornelia give an exclamation and turned to see another police car start its pursuit, and this one switched on the siren as well, a frantic, terrifying sound.

We slipped through the wrought iron boundary fence and burst out into the street. I was losing heart. The car couldn't follow us through the fence, but nothing prevented the cop from getting out and giving chase. Would we be chased on foot through the streets until we were run down and captured? It was *Planet of the Apes,* I thought.

3.

"*I* know where we are," said Cornelia. "Follow me."

We were already halfway up the block when she ran up a driveway between houses and hopped a fence. I followed close behind: more back yards, more fences, more squeezing behind garages. It seemed Cornelia was becoming confused. Now and then I could hear and see the police cars circling the block around us. Once we started over a fence only to be driven back by the sudden appearance of a monster, the harlequin Great Dane, which rose out of the dark and flung itself against the fence, roaring threats. I thought we were moving fast before, but we took off like rabbits, giving no thought to direction, back the way we had come until we were crouched behind a house, gasping for air.

After a time Cornelia straightened up and looked back and forth uncertainly.

"Damn it, I thought I knew where we were. We should have reached it."

I said nothing but let her think.

"We've got to get past that dog," she said.

"If it freaks out again the police will hear it."

"I know. We'll have to go around the front."

It was a ticklish business with the cars still circling, but we managed to steal across a few front lawns and leave the dog behind us. By this time, there was a possibility that some householders might have been awakened and might look out and see us skulking. At the end of the block we stopped and huddled under a big yew bush against the corner house. Time passed and we waited and watched and saw nothing.

Cornelia spoke.

"Now I know where we are. I had the wrong block. We've got to get across that street."

Still we waited. A car rolled down the avenue, but it was not one of our pursuers. At last we felt safe enough to make the dash. I was so tired my eyes were watering. Cornelia led us behind the houses again, then, to my great surprise, straight up the back steps of one house whose first floor windows were brightly lit. She knocked loudly on the back door.

"Masks!" she said suddenly and held out her knapsack. When she had them safely stowed she pounded on the door again and was still knocking when the door was pulled open.

Cornelia walked right in, brushing past the man who had opened the door, pulling me in behind her.

"Cornelia of the Cats. I claim sanctuary. And friend," she added.

We were standing in a narrow kitchen. There were quite a number of men crowded inside. There were bottles on the table and smoke in the air.

The man who let us in looked at us in surprise.

"How many?" he asked.

"Just us two."

"Who's following?"

"Cops."

"Are they close?"

"They might be."

I saw all around me hard faces and sharp eyes turned towards us, some at the table, some looking in through the doorway, all strangers, but all with an unmistakable air of unquestioning welcome. The man who had let us in was a small wiry man with a downturned moustache and unruly hair.

"Come on," he said, and led us to the top of the basement steps.

He handed Cornelia a flashlight.

"You can wait downstairs," he said. "Better wait in the dark. We're just about breaking up here; we can drive you home when we do."

He shut the door above us and we crept down the stairs, with only the steps immediately below our feet lit. We sat on the bottom steps and shut off the light. We heard many voices upstairs, and chairs scraping.

"Who are they?" I asked.

"Geese," said Cornelia. "It's May Day; I knew they'd be awake. Like I told you, drinking and telling stories. They'll take care of us."

This time when she fell asleep on my shoulder I fell asleep right with her. Our heads leaned against each other; her curls made quite a nice pillow. I don't know how long we slept, but we were awakened together, by singing. The Regiment above us were in full voice.

I was enthralled. I awoke to the chorus, a rough-edged union of many voices, unhurried, assured, majestic. Again and again they broke for a new soloist who took up the tale in his own way, then rejoined for their common anthem. It was a tune of great strength, at once an elegy and a boast. I have heard it said that everyone (or every person of regard) remembers the first time he hears *Mo Ghile Mear*. I heard it the first time, sitting in the dark cellar of a strange house with Cornelia of the Cats by my side, roared through the floor above me by the last of the Wild Geese. I have not forgotten it. I didn't know then what they were singing and I have since studied the words and found a lament, but the tune I heard that night spoke a strange joy that could never be taken away by defeat, by misfortune, by anything.

They finished at last, and it was plain that the song was the *pièce de résistance* of the evening for we could hear the party breaking up and the front door opening upstairs. It wasn't long before the light from above shone on us and our host called to us.

"Are you awake? I'll take you home."

He drove an old car, a vintage car perhaps, with long squared-off front and rear hoods. We sat in the back on slippery vinyl seats. I found myself whistling the chorus I had just heard, and our host joined along with me. He knew where Cornelia lived without asking. We were half a block away with only one corner to turn when the man slowed to a crawl and spoke.

"Cornelia. On the south side of the street. In the van, front seat, passenger side. Is he one of yours?"

Cornelia looked back as we turned into her street.

"I don't recognize him. He doesn't look like one of us."

"Not one of mine either, I'm sure of it. But he's on the watch. You'd better tell her."

He let Cornelia off in front of Miss Widdershins' house and she disappeared into the shadows. There were no security lights here.

He drove me home as directed, but instead of letting me out he passed by our house and continued along the block. I was not alarmed, and not surprised when he simply turned around a couple of blocks and came back again, rolling to a stop at our driveway.

"Thanks," I said as I stumbled out the door.

"No trouble, brother."

I was weaving from weariness. I reached in my pocket and found to my relief that the keys to the front door were still inside. When I opened the door, though, I got a nasty shock. The chain was on; there was no way to get in. In those days we used to lock up the house pretty tightly, a relic of the bad old times in New York. I stood exhausted on the porch. I didn't think I had enough energy to climb up to my window. As I tried to think, I heard the chain suddenly slipped off and the door swung open. My sister was standing in her bathrobe and socks. She regarded me with an enigmatic expression.

"You're nuts," was her only comment.

I crawled up the stairs and into my own soft bed.

8. The Letters

1.

There was no question of my going to school next morning. I lay in bed with watering eyes and spasmodic sneezes and refused to move. My parents were always lenient in regard to attendance, and I hadn't missed a day since St. Patrick's, so they didn't press the point. After I fended them off in the early morning I slept until noon.

I lay awake in the bright mid-day room, watching the cracks in the ceiling as I always did and considering the previous night. I laughed at the memory. My mother divined that I was awake and knocked timidly at the door. She asked me how I felt. I could see there was something on her mind. At length, she asked.

"Is everything OK at school? There isn't anyone after you, is there?"

At first I didn't know what she meant. Then I realized she must have thought that there was someone laying for me in school, someone waiting to get me, and that it was fear that kept me home. I laughed in earnest then, and the sound reassured her.

"No, there's no one after me. I'm just tired."

It was a good day. No work to do. I listened to music. I played gin rummy with my grandfather. There were new scratches on my face from hiding in the brambles, but no one mentioned them. Probably they thought I'd gotten the scratches in the fight and they were only now showing themselves as the bruises darkened. The war too ended that day, I recall. Everyone was happy about that.

My sister never said a word. We never told on each other; we were not like some television family. After dinner, though, when we were alone in the living room, she did fix me with a terrible stare and intone the following adaptation from *Great Expectations:* "A boy may lock his door, may be warm in his bed, may tuck himself up, may draw the clothes over his head, may think himself comfortable and safe, but that young woman will softly creep and creep her way to him and tear him open." Not a precise parallel by any means, but it seemed to amuse her.

I was back in school on Friday, and Saturday began my sentence. It was a fine day wasted. All the detainees sat in a classroom for hours, breaking for lunch. The four proud brawlers were there, but I didn't recognize most of the other kids, nor did I know what crimes they had committed. We were allowed to bring homework, and I tried to space mine to last for the whole day. Mostly I daydreamed. At noon we were allowed into the lunch room, and we spread out across the wide open spaces, gathering into little knots separated by empty tables.

At the end of the day I wandered out into the busy Bronx, and somewhat to my surprise found the correct subway station without difficulty. It seemed like a long ride down to Manhattan. The subway always used to give me a headache. When I got to Penn Station I bought a Kung Fu magazine at an underground newsstand, and that cheered me up on the ride back to Queens.

I got home in plenty of time to watch the Kentucky Derby with my father and grandfather. It was a tradition with us to watch the Triple Crown races, although in truth none of us knew much about racing or horses. My father always made gin and tonics with lots of ice cubes, my grandfather's one drink, and I always liked the magical smell of the juniper in the tall sweating glasses.

I only thought to check the drop box after dinner. There was a letter, sure enough.

Dear James,   *May 2*
                                 St. Athanasius' Day

This letter is being brought to you by the good offices of Dolores. I am in disfavor with Aunt Vivien because we *got tangled up with the muskers and had to go to the Geese for help. I am not allowed out this week and you should not come to call on me. I don't think Aunt Vivien is mad at you, however, because you were ensnared by my wiles and are thus blameless. I don't know why they are mad at all because we discovered the watcher in the van, whom they did not know about. They are watching <u>him</u> now and they think he was sent by Con Gone-Away, although I can't think why he would want to watch us at all.*

I hope to be able to see you next week. Dolores will bring you more letters if I learn any more news.

By the way, the man who brought us home is a man of some importance, a company commander and district officer, by the name of Walsh. He's related to McOwen by marriage. I don't know if that's good or bad. I liked him, as much as that matters.

Thank you for coming on the Ride with us. I am sorry it was abbreviated. When I can come out again we can go back down to the park and see how much of it the Dunleavies burned down. Not too much I hope.

Your devoted friend, presently imprisoned,

Cornelia

Our letters must have crossed; I assumed Dolores brought mine back with her, explaining my own prison sentence.

2.

For the next few weeks, we relied on written correspondence. I saved Cornelia's letters; my own are lost to history. It's just as well. I had precious little to say on my own account, as I had settled back in to an ordinary peaceful routine at school, but I did my best to keep my end of the conversation going.

The second letter from Cornelia arrived before the week was out.

Dear James,   *May 7th*
                                 I don't know whose day

Dolores brought your letter back. We are both under sentence! Mine is up at the end of the week. I am sorry that you won't be free for the whole month. That doesn't seem fair, since you were not the aggressing party. I am glad your friend made a stand against that Hayward. I am glad no one was badly hurt. I hope it is not too boring to have to sit in a room all day. I would go crazy. I am going crazy already and I have the whole house to dwell in. It's not so terrible, to tell the truth. Aunt Vivien feels bad about keeping me in so she is being extra nice.

The reason I'm writing is that there is big news. They found out who the Watcher in the van is! But of even greater significance is how they found out. They were afraid that if they tried to follow him, he'd detect them, and he'd never come back. So they called in the Geese for aid. See, some of the Geese are policemen (which is kind of funny when you think about it.) What they did is, they traced the license plate on the van to find out who owns it. Now we know where he lives, and we can keep an eye on him without him noticing. Right now, no one knows why he is watching us. He is just some guy from Jamaica.

I don't know what Aunt Vivien told the Geese about all this. She has to be careful with them. As I may have mentioned to you before, there are those in the Regiment who dispute Aunt Vivien's claim to the sovereignty. It is on account of the fact that she had a brother and in the natural course of things he would have been king. He died very young when they were both little. It is very sad. She misses him still. According to the way the Regiment do things, we should have elected the next king from within the royal family after Arthur died (Arthur was her brother), but the Dragons never bothered to do that. They say they don't need to. That's one reason they want the Black Book back, because it proves their case. It proves precedent. It's stupid anyway. Everyone would have voted for Aunt Vivien.

We have all the windows wide open today and there's a beautiful summer breeze blowing through the house. I can hear a mockingbird singing in the front yard, and in the backyard I hear the sound of swords tinkling where Uncle Thomas and the Twins are practicing. I will see you soon. May is almost one quarter over.

Best wishes,

Rapunzel

The second Saturday was worst than the first. The novelty had worn off, and there was nothing left but endurance. To make matters worse, there was no letter waiting for me when I got home, and I found that Troll had been there during the afternoon to show off his car. He had even taken my sister for a ride.

"It's an old Mustang," she said. "It's kind of a junker, but very cool. It suits him."

I found the next letter on Tuesday the 13th.

Dear James,   *May 12th*
                          Cornelia's Day (It's my Birthday)

Today is my Birthday, as it says above. We had cake and singing and dancing. It was a really nice time. Lots of people were there, some of them I haven't seen for ages. You would have liked it. Lots of presents too!

There has been an interesting and ominous discovery made about the Watcher in the van. (There are actually two of them, they come on different nights.) One of our hunters followed him into the city and found out he is working for an art dealer. Mr. Dillon, that's our new style lawyer, says that most art dealers are also part-time art thieves, so we think we know what he is about. He must be after the painting I showed you on the second floor, that Flanders street scene, which besides being the most beautiful painting is also by a really famous artist. Mr. Dillon says it would be worth millions of dollars if the dealer could get his hands on it. The only way he could possibly know that it's in our house is if Con Gone-Away told him about it. That means he must have told him all sorts of things about us, and probably must have already sold him the other stuff he stole. Aunt Vivien was worried about the Black Book of Leuven, but everyone thinks Con Gone-Away would keep that "as insurance."

That's bad news and Aunt Vivien took it hard. It means Con has gone further away than we thought. It means he has to be dealt with, and maybe the art dealer too. It's going to be hard to keep the others out of this and I will be interested to see who comes to the general audience on the Ides of May. I will write a report.

I hope detention is not too boring for you. There are only three more weeks to go. I could do with a little boredom, myself. It has been <u>too</u> exciting lately.

Your friend,

Cornelia

It seemed that a "general audience" was a regular occurrence on the ides of every month. I recalled the Ides of March, when I had first gone bicycle riding with Cornelia while Miss Widdershins saw a stream of visitors throughout the day, hearing petitions and rendering judgements as I saw now. Cornelia's high expectations of the May audience were not disappointed. I picked up the next letter on Saturday morning and read it in school.

Dear James,   *May 16th*

What a day, yesterday! A delegation of Geese, including Captain Walsh from May Morning, arrived early in the day and stayed in the upper room with Aunt Vivien for a long time. Uncle Thomas was up there too, and both the lawyers, Mr. Dillon and Mr. Dinan. I think they laid it all out for the Regiment, all about Con Gone-Away and the book and the painting and the art thieves. It's going to be interesting to see what happens. They're going to want to shut Con Gone-Away up, for sure. It would be funny if they wind up helping us get the Black Book back, since it might prove Aunt Vivien's right of succession. They've got no choice, though, it would be trouble for them as well as for us. The whole thing makes Aunt Vivien look bad, so she is unhappy.

While they were up in the room, the other petitioners were left waiting downstairs. There were a bunch of them sitting on the row of chairs on our front porch. We had to bring extra chairs out. I brought them tea and lemonade and cakes and tried to put them at their ease with banter. We finally had to open up the sitting room for them. It was exhausting. When she finally started letting them up, it was early evening before the last of them was gone.

The upshot of it all is that there is going to be another council soon. MacOwen himself, that's the Colonel, will be coming in for that one. There should be some Cats there as well. Maybe I'll see some of my family.

I hope you and your family are well. I am looking forward to the eclipse tonight. It is cloudy but I think we should be able to see it pretty well. I love the full moon. I think if I were not a Christian I would worship the moon.

I will see you soon,

Cornelia

I read this little letter more than once as I waited through detention. Each time I finished, I laid the letter on my desk and surreptitiously took stock of my schoolmates and of the proctor, Bellymen all. They had no idea, I thought. None of them knew the world I knew. They couldn't know. They never would.

My father had drawn my attention to the lunar eclipse the night before. We stood in the driveway and watched the clouds slide under the darkening moon. By a strange coincidence, I had been thinking of Cornelia as I watched the moon, and of Miss Widdershins. High over the world, unfettered by law, unaffected by opinion good or ill, beyond the control of man, as it had been since the beginning, beautiful, white, cold … I, too, loved the moon.

3.

1 received the next letter Wednesday morning, on my way out to school. I had a hard time finding the time and leisure to read it. We were getting toward the end of the year, and the atmosphere on the bus and in the school generally, was frenetic. Cornelia had evidently written the letter in haste.

Dear James,   *May 20th*

> *As if we don't have enough trouble! You wouldn't believe what happened. We actually got a visit from the Truant Officer. The real live Truant Officer. She wanted to know why I wasn't in school. Some neighbor must have informed. Aunt Vivien wanted to keep her out on the porch, but Mr. Dillon persuaded her to let the officer in. She asked us all kinds of impertinent questions. I could see Aunt Vivien getting madder and madder. When she gets really mad she kind of glows. You can actually feel it clear across the room. I thought she'd give the order to take the woman's head off. Literally. I don't think the officer noticed anything. It was a good thing the lawyer was there. He was up to the challenge. We told her I*

had just moved to town (true), and that my mother was sick when I left (true, she had a bad cold) and I was staying with Aunt Vivien. We told her we had been home schooling (unfortunately true.) Apparently there is a lot of paperwork you have to fill out if you want to do that. I didn't even know it was allowed. Anyway, this year is almost over, so we would have to submit all the paper and the curriculum and sillybus and everything for next year, by which time I'll be gone anyway. Still, it's never a good thing to be noticed by the authorities. I could hear Aunt Vivien growling to herself like an old mama bear for the rest of the day.

I wish I'd known the Truant Officer was coming ahead of time. I could have pretended to be simple, like Odysseus when they tried to make him go to Troy. I can do that.

No news on that other thing, or when the gathering is to be.

I hope you're doing better than I am.

Cornelia

I looked for Cornelia after Mass on Sunday and caught up with her in the street. It was the first time we had seen each other since the Ride. We chattered for quite a while. She was still thinking about the truant officer. She filled me in on some details. The truant officer had addressed a lot of her questions to Cornelia personally.

"She acted as if she were my friend. You know, concerned for my welfare. Ha! Ha ha ha."

"Have you ever had a visit from a truant officer before?"

"Never. It's okay, Mr. Dillon will take care of it. I'll be gone in the fall anyway."

"I wanted to ask you about that. Are you moving back to Pennsylvania?"

"I'll be going back with my mama, sooner now than I would

have. We move around a lot, James, that's just the way it is."

I was silent for a while.

"I'll be back," Cornelia said. "Don't worry. We won't lose touch."

"I'm glad."

Cornelia looked up the road. Her family had long since walked out of sight.

"I'd better get going," she said. "Another big weekend. "

We parted.

4.

I brooded over my punishment throughout the week, in the light of this new information. Five lost weekends, and Cornelia would be gone soon after that. A suspension would have been so much easier. A suspension is hardly a punishment at all. Properly considered, it would have been a gift.

I opened the next letter on Wednesday morning.

> *Dear James,*   *May 27*
> *St. Augustine of Hippo Day*
> *[The letter was decorated by a*
> *small drawing of a hippopotamus]*
>
> *The date is set. The Gathering will be this Saturday, the last day in May. MacOwen is scheduled to be there. They will be settling the business of Con Gone-Away and the art thief. What I wouldn't give to be a bird in the rafters at that meeting! They won't be meeting at the house. They need a place that isn't watched. There would be too many of them anyway. There is a lodge that the Geese use and they'll be meeting there. It's not that far away. I could walk there but I will have to stay home. I won't be able to sneak out this time. I wish I could see who was attending. That would give me some clue what they're talking about. If you were free you could go and watch them coming in. Do you think you could skip out on your last weekend of detention? I have enclosed a crude map*

to the place, just in case you can.

Good luck on your exams next week. Soon it will be summer and you'll be free.

Cornelia

I had some good news for Cornelia. The last day's detention was commuted to a half day. We were to be released at noon. Depending on when the Gathering was to take place, I might yet be able to reach it. I dropped that information off on Wednesday evening and waited for a reply.

Friday morning I opened the following note on the bus:

Dear James,   *May 29th*
                                     Ascension Thursday

Great news. I don't know how long it takes you to get home, but it just might work. Come straight to our house as soon as you get back. I have an idea.

Cornelia

By the time this letter had reached me, I had had another stroke of luck. Troll had been badgering me for some time about taking a ride in his car, and on Thursday night, at the end of a long conversation between my mother and my aunt, he had called me to the phone again with the question "When are you gonna take a trip in the Mustang?"

I filled him in on my situation, in so far as it involved school, and asked him if he could give me a ride home from the Bronx on Saturday. It would have been an imposition normally, but he was spending half his time in the car or under the hood, and he jumped at the chance. With him driving, I would be at Miss Widdershin's front door well before one, ready for whatever Cornelia had in mind.

9. The Gathering

1.

When I walked out of the front door of my high school shortly after noon, Troll was already parked out front waiting for me.

"DT!" he called, as I approached.

The stream of released prisoners parted around us as I got in the car, the chosen one.

"Is that guy here, the wrestler?"

Troll looked about with curiosity at the passing students. I hesitated to answer; I didn't want Troll starting more trouble. He looked at me.

"What am I gonna do? I just want to see what he looks like."

At length I picked out Heyward, one of the stragglers.

"That's him, the guy with the blue jacket and the bag over one shoulder."

Troll regarded him narrowly.

"Looks like trouble," was his only comment. "Does your friend need a lift?"

"No, he's staying to use the gym."

My high school was situated on the grounds of a college campus, so Troll drove slowly at first, out of respect for the speed bumps. When he left the campus behind, we picked up speed quickly, and we were soon bucketing every which way through the traffic on the Bronx River Parkway.

I made some complimentary remarks about the conveyance and thanked Troll again for picking me up.

"No problem. I was going out for a drive anyway. After I drop you off I'm going out on the Island."

"Isn't this out of your way?"

"I have no way."

As we spun up the Bronx River's exit ramp and forced our way across three lanes of competing street traffic to get to the entrance of the Cross Bronx, Troll broached a new subject.

"I want to drive this all I can now, anyway. I might not have the opportunity for too much longer."

"How come? Do you have to sell it?"

"No, I'm hanging onto it. Move, move, move! But I might be on Parris Island by the end of the summer."

I was shocked. The thought of Troll taking orders shocked me.

"Really? Wow, when did you decide this?"

"I haven't decided anything, hence the use of the term 'might.' It's something I've been thinking of. I don't think college is right for me."

"What do your parents think?"

"They're thrilled," said Troll dryly. "I don't think they take it quite seriously yet. I've been the court jester so long I don't think anyone believes I can make a serious decision."

"How long have you been thinking about this?"

Troll was not the type of person to run off and join the War on Terror in a sudden excess of patriotism.

"On and off, since I was a kid. I guess I always thought I'd find my way into the armed services eventually, and now with college staring me in the face …"

I absorbed this new information. I didn't have much to offer. Troll pointed out some recruitment literature in the back of the car, and I pored over it. I tried to comment on it in an encouraging manner. Troll in the Marines. Maybe it could work, I thought. Everybody has to do something.

We were soon off the bridge and nearing my house.

"Could you do me a favor," I asked. "Could you drop me off at my friend Cornelia's house?"

"I gotta chauffeur you to your girlfriend's house?" Troll demanded in mock outrage.

"She's not my girlfriend."

"Please! Please. You're embarrassing us both."

Troll got mixed up in the dead end streets when he anticipated my directions, but we were still in front of Miss Widdershin's house before a quarter to one.

"Could you do me one more favor?"

"You want me to wait here?"

"Yes."

"Oh, sure."

Cornelia must have been watching for me. By the time I got to the front steps she was opening the screen door. She had left the door of the house half open and I could sense figures moving around inside. She came to the bottom step and bent her head close to me.

"You got here fast," she whispered. "There's still time. Do you have that map I drew you?"

I did, and it was all that I had. I was traveling light, in anticipation of Cornelia's "idea."

"Take this." She fumbled a cell phone to me. "Do you know how to use one of these?"

"Yes."

"I taped my number to the back." She flashed her corresponding phone. "Here's what you do. Get to some place outside the lodge where you can see the people going in. Then call me up and describe them."

I considered this.

"When are they starting?"

"Now. Chop chop."

Someone walked out on the porch. I heard the boards creak.

"Gotta go."

When she reached the top of the stairs, she called over her shoulder, "Some other time, then."

Back in the car, Troll addressed me with indignation.

"She's cute. Why don't you just admit she's your girlfriend? Just say it. You'll feel better."

I groaned. I had too much on my mind to come up with a clever retort.

"Take it from me, in a couple of years, she's gonna become a fox. That kind always does."

I smirked a little, remembering that, one month ago to the day, Cornelia had become a fox of a somewhat different kind.

"Could you do me one more …"

"Where?"

It was only a five-minute drive. I had Troll drop me a couple of blocks from the lodge, so I could make an inconspicuous approach.

"Thanks, man." I said. "You did me a solid."

"Don't you forget it, my brother."

We exchanged a complicated handshake, a humorous reconstructed relic of the seventies. He never did ask me what I was up to.

2.

The "Lodge" was on the edge of one of those odd little miniature business districts that are sprinkled throughout Queens. When I saw the layout, some peculiarities of Cornelia's map were made clear to me. The lodge was a solid old brick building, set back from the road. It could only be reached by a long narrow driveway that ran past a smaller wooden house which gave the impression of being a guardhouse. It was all private property. There were a number of buildings clustered together in a haphazard way. It was a grouping that must have been assembled a long time ago. Nowadays, the strict rule of Real Estate would have forbidden such an arrangement. It was practically a compound.

As I approached the area on foot, a flaw in Cornelia's plan became apparent. If I were simply to stand in the street, watching the councilors arrive and reporting into my cell phone, there was a very good chance that I would be seen and noticed. There were a number of Dragons who knew me by sight. I could imagine being transfixed by an angry glance from Miss Widdershins as she walked to the meeting. Would someone be dispatched to deal with me?

I found some cover across the street. There was an ice cream parlor with tables set outside. I could sit at a table and watch the comings and goings across the way in relative obscurity. There were umbrellas standing over the tables as well, a welcome bonus as the clouds were beginning to darken. By one o'clock I was seated at a sidewalk table, nursing a chocolate malt and trying to figure out how to use the cell phone. I had never had an occasion to use a cell phone before, and I had some trouble with the buttons initially. It turned out to be quite simple. It was one of those throwaway cell phones that you buy without a contract.

"Hello, Cornelia?"

I huddled over the phone. Traffic noise was going to be a problem.

"It's me. Where are you?"

"I'm in position across the street."

"Can you see the Lodge?"

"I can see the entranceway."

"Any action?"

"Some guy walked up the driveway while I was getting my ice cream. He was a tall black guy in a grey suit. Charcoal grey. Kind of a slim guy with big shoulders. He looks like he's about thirty."

"I know who that is, although I've never seen him. He's older than he looks. That's Emile Stokowsky. He's a solicitor for the Geese."

"Stokowsky?"

"He's Haitian," Cornelia explained.

I had to let that go, for there were other people arriving.

"Hey, I recognize someone. It's Walsh, the guy who drove us home on May Day."

"It's right that he should be here. He's district officer. Also, he discovered the guy in the van. Is he alone?"

"There are a couple of people with him. Jackets and ties. Long moustaches. They might be the two guys who came to your aunt's door that time."

"They might."

"I don't see your aunt anywhere."

"Probably she's already inside, seated at the head of all the tables."

"There's a little red-haired woman, kind of plumpish, in a long flowery ornate dress. She's turning into the driveway now. She's got a tall bald guy walking with her with grey hair and a pointy beard.'"

"I know who that is. That's Aunt Vivien's cousin Cassie. I didn't know she was in town. I'm glad she's here. They are great friends. Did you say 'plumpish'?"

"She looks very pretty," I amended.

"We're all very pretty, James. The goatee guy is her husband Donnchadh, that's Duncan. He collects antique weapons. They're both able dancers, too, for all she's so plump. Who else?"

"Someone just came out of the house and up the driveway. He's about middle height, middle build. Short hair. He looks like he's maybe in his forties, maybe older. He's in dark clothes with a dark jacket, not a suit. He's got a dark look altogether. He's walking all the way up the driveway. He's looking for someone. He looks like he's in charge. He looks dangerous."

"You have seen MacOwen, the commander of the Geese throughout all the world. He can call on his people from six continents. A man of great wisdom and deep purpose. It is he who is contesting the sovereignty with Aunt Vivien, though not on his own behalf. For all that, though, he will stand or fall with the rest of us. Is anyone with him?"

"One guy. A younger guy, kind of a muscle guy in short sleeves. He looks a little hyper."

"I don't know who that is unless it's MacQuillan, one of his guards. From what I've heard he's a lot hyper. I am surprised he's at such a tricky difficult meeting."

"They're waiting for someone. Hey, it's one of the twins. He's conducting a little guy with a big nose and long grey hair pulled back. The little guy has his arms full of papers. He's wearing little wire-rimmed glasses,"

"That's Mr. Dinan, our old style lawyer! He'd have to be there."

"They're all going in now."

"Anyone else?"

"I don't see anyone."

"No Cats?"

"Maybe they're inside already?"

Cornelia said nothing. I sipped the bottom of my malt, opening the lid and poking the last solid clump of ice cream with my straw. I was ready to hang up.

"Wait, a car is rolling up in front. A big old maroon car. Two people are getting out, a man and a woman. They're both tall, fast. They look like they're in a hurry."

"Describe them."

"The woman is slender, she has longish black hair. She's got a plaid skirt; she moves like a dancer. The man's bigger, about the same height. He's wearing some sort of fancy paisley vest over a long sleeved shirt. They're younger than the others. They're gone already. They were laughing."

"Is the car still there? Quick, look at the plates."

"I can't see them. Wait, it's pulling away." I got up and walked to the sidewalk. "Pennsylvania."

"Thought so. They're Cats, the chief's son and daughter, Donald and Mary. They're a lot of fun, especially Mary. That's probably the last of them. The Cats are always last minute."

I waited for a while, but Cornelia proved correct. No one else arrived.

"One last thing," Cornelia said. "When no one's looking, throw your phone away."

"Wouldn't it be a good idea to hang on to it?"

"No, we always throw our phones away after a month or so. I rescued these two from the garbage. And don't forget to pull off the tape with my number."

"OK."

"Thanks, you've given me a lot to think about. Over and out."

We never did learn exactly what went on in that council, but we tried to piece it together over the next few weeks. Cornelia was sure that there had been no debate about the sovereignty and Miss Widdershins' right to it. She said that the Cats would never have sent Donald and Mary if that were the matter in question, but the chief himself would have come. They must only have been present as observers, to carry news back to their family.

"When I was a little girl," she added, "I used to follow Mary everywhere, like a little puppy dog. I even used to dress like her. I haven't seen her for a long time. I wonder if she'll stop by the house before she goes back home."

She filled me in on a few of the other figures I had seen.

"Aunt Vivien's cousin Cassie is her aunt's daughter on her father's side, that's the old King. She's probably her best friend."

I tried to draw the lines in my head.

"Do you know what Cassie is short for?" she asked confidentially. "Cassibellauna!"

She chuckled.

"I got off easy with Cornelia!"

Then she added more thoughtfully, "I wonder. Her husband Duncan is a collector. Antique weapons, antique furnishings, antique this-and-that. I wonder if he was there to give an opinion on the art dealer. He might know something about him. He might even know him."

Back at the Widdershins household no one was giving much away. Cornelia kept her ears open – "I know better than to ask questions," she said – but there were only scattered clues. She said that her aunt seemed better pleased with the tenor of the council than she had expected to be.

"There wasn't any nonsense," Cornelia heard her say. "MacOwen must have his own worries with his own people. I suppose I shouldn't take comfort in that, but it means he hasn't the standing or the inclination to trouble me."

To me, the surprise was that nothing much seemed to have

changed. I expected a big decision and decisive action. Instead, the house seemed to sink into a comfortable routine, as one lazy summer day followed the next. I couldn't understand why there was no urgency. I thought that Con Gone-Away and his accomplice were considered an open threat to all the tribes, to their secret lives in their secret kingdoms. Cornelia and I puzzled over this question in earnest whispers and at length decided that their enemies' greed must render them less immediately dangerous. As long as Gone-Away and the Dealer had hopes of acquiring the painting, and perhaps other equally marvelous treasures we didn't know about, any interference by outsiders would have been contrary to their interests. If they were to gain and keep the prize, this was a duel that would have to be fought in private.

One change we did notice: the Geese were now frequently at the house, and they entered easily into the daily life of the court. It was fascinating to me to observe the subtly different way they related to the Dragons and to Miss Widdershins especially. They were a little like a branch of the family that we hadn't seen for a long while, well-remembered by some, less so by others, invited to the reunion or to the wedding, and all determined to be as friendly and as welcoming as they could be. Whereas the Dragons were as familiar to one another as children of the same parents, there were new angles of relationship to calculate now between each new visitor and each set of hosts.

Miss Widdershins was still undisputed queen of her court; if anything, the Geese were more obviously deferential than even her own proper subjects. Still, by their very politeness they bore witness to a new distance. The atmosphere was not strained, everyone knew their steps well enough, but where there was once perfect unity, now there was a constant reminder of an outside influence and of the authority to which the members of the Regiment also owed allegiance.

From an observation of the movements of the Geese, and from overhearing parts of the messages they brought and received, Cornelia and I concluded that each party had its own sphere of action. The Geese seemed to be concerned purely with the Art Dealer and his minions. We guessed that their access to police and legal resources would make it easier for them to learn what they needed to learn and to do what they needed to do. The matter of Con Gone-Away and the Black Book was left to the Dragons to settle.

There was little obvious increase in security at the house. That was left to the Dragons too. A few new faces popped up, and there were always men about the house now even when the twins and Thomas were out, but the place never took on the look of an armed camp.

10. The Cookout

1.

The next week closed out the semester and my freshman year. I got through my exams without too much trouble. My outside interest absorbed most of my mental energy, which made me less inclined to study, but also less inclined to worry uselessly. The summer opened with a rainy laborious Saturday. By some chain of events I have now forgotten, it had been decided that our house would be the site of a large family gathering on Sunday. Someone may have been graduating from something. I don't know why our house was selected. Maybe the natural hosts were having renovations done. Maybe it was just our turn.

While my mother was a naturally hospitable person, she was prey to fearsome bouts of anxiety whenever we had guests over in any numbers. In this case, worry was intensified by the bad weather; it looked like the gathering would have to be held inside our small house. That meant guests milling around while she was cooking, instead of the much easier cookout overseen by my father, and it also meant fielding the constant criticisms directed at our home and furnishings. We had an old house, with little old bathrooms and a little old kitchen, and we were content with it. Our doors creaked, our windows stuck, our linoleum was riven by strange rents, our front door rattled, the steam knocked loud in the radiators, the upstairs hall light had a trick to it, the numbers were worn off the stove. When we were alone at home we noticed none of it; we simply adapted and flowed around all obstacles. I don't know why we were like this, unless it was that each of us lived mostly in his own imagination. Our relatives were scandalized by these shortcomings, and scandalized anew every time they visited. We were happy enough with things as they were, but the repetitious unwelcome raillery grew tedious.

That moist Saturday my sister, my father and I went out on many missions to many stores while my mother cleaned the house. Even my grandfather pitched in as best he could; he was feeling a little better now that he was getting over his spring cold. My parents quarreled, as my father thought that my mother was undertaking over-elaborate cleaning projects. It was a relief when we all settled down in front of the television in the late afternoon to watch the Belmont Stakes, in a room calmed by the faint perfume of gin.

"It feels good to put my feet up," said my mother.

My father suddenly groaned.

"Do you hear that?" he demanded. He pointed the remote and pressed it. "Listen!"

The sounds of "New York, New York" filled the room.

"That's what they play now," he said. "It used to be 'The Sidewalks of New York,' a lovely old nostalgic nineteenth-century tune that fit in perfectly with the others. It was 'My Old Kentucky Home,' 'Maryland, My Maryland' and the 'The Sidewalks of New York.' A bit of old New York. They had to get rid of that, of course, so now we have to listen to this glitzy vulgarian Las Vegas show-biz boast."

"That's the way with everything," said my mother.

"Listen to that: 'If I can make it there …' Gotta make it. Everyone's gotta make it."

He stopped suddenly and laughed.

"Success is the opiate of the middle class," he said. "Never mind. Let's watch the race."

It was a good race. Once more the winner of the first two races was turned back on the verge of winning the Triple Crown. We were disappointed, but happy.

After dinner, when my sister played the piano, my father brought a request to her and with it an old red music book from my grandfather's high school days. He propped it open on the piano over her sheet music. We gathered around and looked over her shoulder, trying to read the words of the verses and all joining in on the chorus:

Eastside, Westside, all around the town
Tots sing Ring a Rosy, London Bridge is Falling Down
Boys and girls together
Me and Mamie O'Rourke
We tripped the lights fantastic
On the sidewalks of New York.

2.

Sunday was cloudy, but there was no rain. The cookout was back on. My parents relaxed. The guests arrived piecemeal and drifted outside.

"James, why don't you get your friend The Toad to help you bring some more chairs into the backyard?"

"Please, Uncle John, Troll."

We rooted around inside the house for chairs suitable for lawn service. Our back steps were a little uneven, the work of a handyman unerringly selected by my grandfather, and Troll stumbled on his way down and let fall a kitchen chair in the mud.

He dropped to his knees.

"I have disgraced myself. Please kill me. Somebody please kill me."

Troll was a devotee of Samurai movies and he had recently seen a film where one of the characters made just such a plea in attempted expiation of some fault. It had charmed Troll and he added the phrase to his repertoire. It became a catchphrase at that cookout, to the great amusement of Troll, my sister and myself, and to the increasing irritation of everyone else. It was the "Kill Me" cookout.

I brought two chairs to my second cousins, Jane and Anna. They were a couple of years older than I, and came from farther out on The Island. I only knew them slightly; they seemed to me then to be figures of great sophistication and elegance. I think it was Anna who was graduating that year. I was bashful in their presence. I look at photos now from that cookout, and they look like bright–eyed mischievous children. Still, I don't think my original impression was completely in error. My sister liked talking to them, and pulled her chair close. They did not "get" Troll.

People fished for beers. Cooked hamburgers began finding their way onto buns.

"How can you not have broadband?"

"I don't understand the question," said my father, standing at the grill.

"How can you stand dealing with dial up?"

"I only read emails. It's fast enough."

"What about your kids? Pretty soon all school assignments are going to require use of the Internet."

"Their grades are adequate."

"That's not the point. There's a whole different way of learning now. What are they going to do when they get to college?"

"I am not impressed by the impact of the Internet on people's ability to reason. I've seen it. Fewer and fewer people can even follow a narrative. It's all bits and pieces."

"It's non-linear. Hypertext driven. The impact of the Internet on communication is going to be greater that the impact of print. In a few years, all research is going to be done online. People who don't keep up with the technology are going to be left out. Even the newspapers are dying. How are you going to know what's going on?"

"I'd rather be ignorant than stupid," my father said.

I heard my sister guffaw.

"That should be our family motto," she said.

My father passed a hamburger off to the Internet booster and he found a seat next to my grandfather. I pitied him if he hoped to continue the conversation there. My grandfather was still asking people where the Internet was. The company moved their seats into a rough circle. Anna was questioned about her future plans, and answered composedly about a pre-med program. I was impressed; I think we all were.

The cookout was moving along like any other cookout, until I became conscious of a face peeking around our high wooden fence. My mother was a half step ahead of me.

"Cornelia! Come and join us. James, Cornelia is here."

Cornelia remained shyly in the driveway. I felt oddly awkward as I walked over to her, under the eyes of my extended family.

"Come on in," I said to her when I reached her. "We're having hamburgers."

"I didn't know you had company today."

She peeped around me at the guests as we walked back to a couple of open seats. My mother assisted with introductions. Friendly faces were turned to us. Troll raised his eyebrows and regarded me knowingly. Everyone seemed to be pleasantly amused at me, for some reason. For a while Cornelia parried some easy questions of the "where do you live," "where do you go to school," "do you want something to eat" variety. She had learned to dismiss the school question with the magic words "home schooled" which were just then beginning to be widely recognized. In time the party shifted its interest elsewhere, and Cornelia and I were left to our own conversation. We soon gave up any attempt to discuss the gathering of the tribes on the previous Saturday. Cornelia observed my relatives with great interest and listened hard to their conversations, which joined and broke up and amalgamated and spun off all across the yard.

"We're having a big gathering too at the house. I just nipped out to take a break. They were getting a little noisy."

"So you wound up stuck here at our gathering instead."

"That's OK. I like it. Do you always do this for Pentecost, too?"

"No, no. It's just a graduation celebration. My cousin Anna is graduating from high school, that's the blonde girl over there. You have parties for Pentecost?"

"Since forever. Everyone comes to court. It's supposed to be a good time for starting missions and adventures. And telling stories. It's a good time to ask for favors, too."

I was surprised to find her away from the house on a day like that, and told her so.

"Maybe this is my adventure," she said, and became interested in my Aunt Kate, who was passing around pictures from her Easter vacation in Florida.

"Look at the bank of the pool. Do you see that? It's hard to see. That's an eight-foot gator."

"Let me see that," said my Aunt Denise, Jane and Anna's mother. "Oh my gosh, where is that?"

"It's a golf course in Naples. There are gators all over the place down there. I mean all over the place, any body of fresh water you have to watch out."

"Are there any geese in there?" asked Aunt Denise. Then, looking at another picture, "There are! Alligators and geese, just like the song!"

"Eh?" My grandfather was conscious that he was missing something.

"There used to be a song way back when, when we were in college," explained my Aunt Kate. "All about alligators and geese, and Noah's Ark. Do you remember that?" She began singing the chorus.

Other voices joined in the song. Many other voices.

"Remember that?"

"You used to hear it all the time."

"Do you remember the gestures?"

Aunts Denise and Kate stood up and began to demonstrate. There were signs for the animals. Everyone laughed and remembered.

"You used to do that," said my Aunt Kate nodding to her husband, Uncle Robert, the champion of broadband. She had detected a little too much mockery in his laughter.

"I never did the gestures."

"Oh, yes you did. I remember distinctly. We had just started going out, and we were at the Minstrel Boy, and I was afraid you were too much of a serious young business type. Then when I saw you bopping around to the music, I thought maybe there was a chance for you after all. The rest is history. So have some respect!"

Cornelia listened carefully to all this. She then contrived to piece almost the entire song together by questioning the most knowledgeable of my relatives. When she had collected the song to her satisfaction, she asked, "But where did it come from?"

"Who knows? The Irish Rovers used to do it."

"It's 'The Unicorn,' by Shel Silverstein," said my father, who up until then had not taken part in the conversation. "Shel Silverstein. He's a children's author with a big beard. He wrote *The Giving Tree.*"

Cornelia nodded and repeated the name. For a while she withdrew from her surroundings and I could see her running through the words quietly.

My father started up another round of burgers. When the time was ripe, Troll came up for his third.

"I've been meaning to ask you," said my father. "That shirt. What is the 'Three-Fold Path?' What are you, a Buddhist now? No, I suppose not," that last bit added as he passed him the juicy hamburger.

"Don't ask him," warned my Aunt Joanne. "Do not ask him."

It was too late.

"I am glad you inquired, Uncle John," began Troll. He stretched his tan shirt better to display a small, tastefully-lettered legend, 'The Three-Fold Path.' On the back of the shirt was a large blue spoked wheel, like an old-time captain's wheel. "The Three-Fold path is a path to enlightenment discovered by myself and certain associates of mine."

"I can't listen to this again." Aunt Joanne actually rose and moved away.

"And what is this path to enlightenment based on?"

"Strangely enough on William Shatner. Specifically, on William Shatner's performance of the song 'Rocket Man.' "

"I should have listened to your mother."

"Attend. You are no doubt aware of Shatner's legendary performance of 'Rocket Man' at the 1978 Science Fiction Film Awards. A friend of mine discovered a copy on the web, and we used to view it obsessively. Eventually it became clear to us that there was a message in there for those who would listen. Let me refresh your memory. It begins with Shatner sitting in a chair, smoking a cigarette, ultra cool, speaking the lines with kind of a sardonic hipster intonation. Then halfway through, a second Shatner appears behind him and starts speaking. He's not super cool, he speaks with this air of dramatic wonderment, wide-eyed. See, already that teaches us that coolness is not the ultimate, you have to recapture the wonder. Then finally a third Shatner appears, with his tie undone, rocking, zonked out on cocktails, wild, free. Now that looks like the goal, what we call Dynamic Nirvana, but it's not the end. This is important. At the end all three Shatners are integrated. They recombine into one man. And that's the goal. A totally integrated personality. Following the three stages."

"And what happens when you reach that goal?"

"Presumably you die. There's nothing further in this world for you. You are released from the wheel of rebirth. Your soul is free."

"How come Shatner isn't dead?"

"We've thought about that. We believe God keeps him here as an example to others."

"I'd think some more."

Troll turned to me.

"I could show you the clip right now. It will blow your mind. Oh, wait I'm sorry. I can't. I forgot you have dial up. And now I've shamed you in front of your guests, after enjoying your hospitality. I have disgraced myself. Please kill me."

"One of these days," said my father, "somebody's going to take you up on that."

"*Quo usque tandem?*" asked my grandfather. Then, by way of explanation, "*Quo usque tandem abutere Eugeni patientia nostra?* How long, Cataline – or in this case, Eugene – will you continue to abuse our patience? That's Cicero's first oration against Cataline. We had to memorize the first part of it in school. It seemed à propos. *Quam diu etiam furor iste tuus nos eludet?* How long will your madness bedevil us? "

I noticed even then that my grandfather's occasional forays into Latin caused a ripple of embarrassment throughout the rest of the family. I have since concluded that they constituted a slightly shameful reminder of our parochial roots, of the shabby ghetto from which we had all, supposedly, struggled to emerge, and which we were all anxious to forget.

Troll broke a brief silence by answering my grandfather.

"A long time, I'd say. A long time."

My Aunt Denise leaned forward and addressed Cornelia.

"I bet you little dreamed when you came over here that we're all crazy."

Cornelia responded with her usual secret smile, which was mostly a response to her own hidden thoughts.

"You should see my family."

The party started breaking up. Everyone had places to go, Cornelia among them. On his way out, my Uncle Robert asked my grandfather.

"When are you going to get this place painted?"

My grandfather looked around in surprise.

"Does it need painting?"

"Are you kidding? The paint is worn totally off some of the shingles. I can see the wood. And look at the windowsills."

The windows and sills were shedding white paint in thick flakes.

"I guess you're right."

"Even if you don't care how it looks, you save money in the long run if you keep it painted. You're probably going to have to replace a lot of those shingles."

"They're cedar shake," said my father. "They don't rot."

"If they're wood, they rot."

"Dad, in forty years here, how many shingles have you lost?"

"I don't think …"

"You're not seriously telling me you don't think this place needs a paint job badly."

"No. I'm not telling you that. It needs painting."

That answer seemed to satisfy him. At any rate, he left.

We ferried the leftovers into the house and folded up the card tables. It was a pleasant gathering, but it would take a couple of days for us to recover. My mother was most strongly affected. She enjoyed having guests, but the effort of hospitality, especially for large gatherings, wore her down. We were all in the same predicament to varying degrees.

My mother asked my grandfather, "What were you talking to Eugene about? I saw the two of you cloistered together for some time."

"He wanted to ask me about military life. His mother wanted me to speak to him too. I don't know what good I did him. I was in the service sixty years ago. I wasn't a Marine. And we didn't volunteer."

"He really wants to join the Marines? He's still just a big kid."

"So were we. They take all kinds. All the same, I hope he doesn't do it."

"Fighting for strangers," said my father.

My grandfather grunted an assent.

After everything was cleared away, my father stood with his hands in his pockets looking around the backyard. His gaze fell on our garage, on the fading shingles nearest the ground.

"I suppose it needs a painting," he said sadly.

On each of the shingles the dulled blue-gray of the house paint wore away toward the bottom, where the flat color of the wood was painted with a hundred subtle variations of green and brown laid on by the sun and rain, paper-thin moss worked into the crevices, the tea stains of wet oak leaves, each shingle a unique and ever-changing composition of unresisted time. I knew then that my father did not resent the money spent on a paint job or even the intrusion into our lives that would be made by the work crews, he simply regretted what would be lost, the haphazard beauties left by decay, covered up by thick uniform unvarying coats of paint.

My father was captivated by what one could call the aesthetics of happenstance. Even when he worked on the yard, when he cleared away weeds or ivy, he could not resist leaving some behind to ruin the smooth perfection that others valued, although he knew it would only spread again. The shape of our backyard, the succession of wild flowers that sprouted and then died leaving only their browning leaves behind, sprang from my father's disinclination to interfere with the private doings of nature, except by occasional encouragement. There was an old concrete and slate path in our backyard that had been broken up long ago by the grinding of an earth mover. When our neighbors were building their new house, we had let the earth mover pass through our yard to get at the areas they could not otherwise reach. The great metal treads had made a hash of our old footpath. It was now broken through in many places, heaving up out of the level here and there, with thick vegetation growing through the cracks, a hazard to the unwary. Everyone thought that my father left it that way, without repairing or replacing it, out of sheer cheapness, but I knew that he liked it that way. It reminded him of a ruin. No wonder he found it difficult to talk to other people.

11. The Wine-Bibbers

1.

It rained a lot over the next week. When I saw Cornelia in such conditions it was usually at my house, and we usually sat and watched television while the big raindrops beat the worn metal top of the window air conditioner. There was no television at Miss Widdershins' house, and my impression was that Cornelia didn't watch much TV back in Pennsylvania either. Since it was all new to her, she arrived with no favorites, and watched whatever I put on. On weekends we watched a lot of sports, while during the week it was mostly DVDs. We had an eclectic collection to say the least, everything from Cagney to Schwarzenegger. She seemed to enjoy it all, watching with scientific interest.

"I never watch at home," she said. "Aunt Vivien calls it Cailitín's box. She says it fills men's minds with groundless fears."

The Children of Cailitín, Cornelia explained to me, were six witches who were corrupted by Queen Maeve and raised to lure Cú Chulainn out of the Glen of the Deaf by projecting on his mind the terrible sounds and images of illusory foes. He sallied forth out of season, when the Men of Ulster were still in their pains, to defend his country against a danger that was real only to him, and so he was entrapped and destroyed.

"Aunt Vivien thinks that it draws people into a shadow world, and they spend their lives dealing with and worrying about and grasping at things that aren't real."

"We call it the boob tube and the idiot box," I said. "But we still watch it."

When I visited the Widdershins house in the rain, Cornelia and I usually played games in the basement. We played chess, checkers, shut the box, and once we even took part in a grand experiment, whereby we, along with Uncle Thomas, were enlisted by Miss Widdershins to help her learn to play bridge.

"I read in many books where the generality of people in your society play bridge. They seem to derive great satisfaction from it. I would like to learn how it is played. Let us take advantage of the rain to make the attempt."

I vividly remember her seated at the head of the dining room table, peering through little gold-rimmed granny glasses at her cards, and making a little thoughtful tipping sound with her tongue between her lips. Then she would tilt over in her chair and consult an open book at her side.

"I don't know what this means," she would say at last. "Thomas, what does this mean?"

He would dutifully look at the book and they would thrash the matter out until they came up with a solution which I am sure had little to do with bridge as it was played beyond those four walls. Cornelia would rise and stand behind them and offer absurd suggestions.

The attempt to play the game was a complete fiasco, but the afternoon to my mind was a great success. I noticed that Cornelia never seemed to lack for free time during the summer, although I don't suppose that her home schooling followed the same on-again off-again fall-summer pattern that the regular school year followed. I think Miss Widdershins was giving us all the time together that we could use, since she must have known that very soon there would be no time at all. She spent more of her own time with us as well. She must have been glad of the distraction, as the house more and more became the haunt of grim-faced men with trouble on their minds. The atmosphere was never allowed to remain grim for long when Miss Widdershins was about. As the time of trial came, she became more serene, and even playful, and she drew all others into her charmed circle. It was *noblesse oblige*, I suppose.

2.

At length the rains cleared away for a good long spell of sun, and we found ourselves facing the first real heat of the new summer. It was on St. John the Baptist's Day, as Cornelia would have said, that I walked over to join a throng of courtiers in Miss Widdershins' backyard. I heard the hubbub of voices from the street. By that time, I was easy enough in manner with them that I walked down the driveway into the yard without bothering to knock or announce myself. I heard the brisk light ring of steel while I was still wending my way through the cars parked in the drive.

I saw Thomas walking the strange circle again, with a long swept hilt rapier shining in his hand. This time he had a partner who walked with him, Miss Widdershins, facing him across the circle with a cup hilt rapier of her own. Throughout the yard were scattered Dragons and Geese, regarding the exhibition with varying degrees of attention.

Both players were encased in full fencing gear. Both wore what looked to be dark brown breastplates of hardened leather, with long padded sleeves and thick fencing tights. It must have been punishingly hot inside those uniforms. Although her face, like her partner's, was completely covered by a dark helmet, there was no mistaking Miss Widdershins' hourglass figure beneath the covering. The effect was spoiled somewhat by a short puffy skirt that she wore over it all, in what was no doubt a concession to an archaic concept of modesty. In the ensemble she looked like some brazen goddess of war brought to life, as envisioned by Ray Harryhausen.

The fencing was genteel in manner. It seemed to be a drill rather than a contest. They crossed swords at a distance, both standing very upright and holding their arms almost straight, passing the tips over or under the other's blade in turn, until, on some hidden signal, one stepped forward and bent the foiled blade on the other's protected breast. All the time they were doing this, they stepped around the circle, orbiting around the center, and moving across only to deliver an attack. The swords shone like silver when they passed beneath a gap in the leaves above. I watched for a while, until I saw Cornelia on the other side of the ring, beckoning to me.

Soon I had passed through the gauntlet of glances and was seated in the grass alongside Cornelia, watching the display.

"Spanish fencing. Old style. Uncle Tom's new hobby," she explained.

I had never seen Miss Widdershins out of her long dresses. I watched her sturdy dark-clad legs as she stepped. A strong woman indeed, I thought. At length, she stopped, held up her left hand and stamped twice. They both relaxed. She pulled off her helmet with some difficulty. Her thick hair was tied into a golden braid. Her face glowed with sweat.

"Enough," she said. "I'm cooked in here."

Her partner emerged from his cocoon as well. He had long ago shaved off his side whiskers and adopted the bullet-head haircut of the rest of them. He gave a salute, which she returned.

"Thanks for stepping it out with me," he said. "I think we're getting the hang of it."

"Dolores," Miss Widdershins called to her lady's maid. "Help me out of this."

The little woman rose from her seat and they walked together up into the house.

I took the opportunity to look around at the other people. There were a few new faces, among them the Haitian lawyer, nattily attired in a grey suit as he had been on the day of the gathering. Across the yard, Balin was helping Thomas unbuckle his protective gear.

"I just don't see the use of it, unless you're challenged to a formal duel," he was saying.

"It's an art form. It doesn't need a use. Besides, it teaches angles, body displacement."

A voice nearer to me spoke quietly.

"Thomas the Rhymer. Did you ever fence with him?"

The questioner was one of the new faces, an unknown Goose, a lean man with a seamed red face. He was speaking to the Haitian lawyer.

"Oh, yes, we frequently bouted when we were both stationed in St. Augustine the one winter."

"How'd you do?"

"Quite well. It was Olympic fencing. My weapons, not his. Also, you must understand, he is not really a fencer. When he fences with you he is seldom trying to beat you. He is observing you."

A small knot of men had gathered around the now unarmored swordsman to heft and flex the rapiers and to prove the toughness of the leather covering in various ways. Cornelia had left my side, and I saw her walking over to her uncle with a big pitcher of lemonade and a glass. She was wearing a dark blue dress, decorated by small white flowers. There was a dark blue beret, in shape like a Glengarry, nesting comfortably in her hair. The others made room for her; I got the impression that they regarded her with a certain fondness.

"*Comme la Fille du Régiment,*" murmured the Haitian.

Her uncle tossed off a long draught. I sat on the grass and observed the people around me. No one seemed to mark my presence. I tried to listen in on snatches of conversation. Mostly they spoke English, with one or two odd words thrown in, enough to confuse my ear from time to time. In at least one case, a couple of men were sawing away earnestly in a frankly foreign tongue, and I couldn't understand a word. Cornelia's language lessons had proved, as I had foreseen, almost entirely useless. She would occasionally come out with Fun Facts like, "these are called kippies," holding up a match, or "we call them preachers," pointing to a crow, but there was no sustained effort to teach me the language. As it turned out, I wouldn't have had the time to learn.

Cornelia came and sat by my side, and we both sipped lemonade. She folded her legs under her dress, which spread about her on the dark grass. As I took stock of the company I saw there were fewer present than I had at first thought. There were no young people, aside from myself and my companion. There were never any young people.

At length Miss Widdershins reappeared, clad in a very plain pale blue dress, with Dolores in tow. She stood on the landing at the top of the stoop as she liked to do, and surveyed her people.

Cornelia walked to the foot of the stairs, and I followed. Miss Widdershins' attention was captured by an animated argument that was being conducted by Thomas and one of the Geese, the brick-colored man who had been talking to Emile the Haitian lawyer earlier. They seemed to be arguing politics, apportioning blame between a man named Sullivan and a man named Murray. I was not familiar with either. Miss Widdershins listened with growing annoyance.

"I suppose things would have gone differently had you been there," she interjected.

Thomas inclined his head with a smile.

"Of course, of course."

"And yet there were some good men present all the same."

"Do you know that the Bellymen believe in an infinite number of alternate universes, an endless number of other worlds where every conceivable alternative really happens? I have heard them say so," said the brick-faced man. "So in some other universe we did win and the prince was restored."

"And in still other universes there was no prince, no kingdom and presumably no earth or sun at all. I have heard about such things. I can't believe it."

"No no, of course not."

"I mean I cannot believe that anyone else believes it. Not even the Fir Bullug."

"Maybe there is a duplicate Vivien in some other universe who does believe it," suggested Thomas.

Miss Widdershins gave a wry smile.

The only reason I remember this exchange is that Cornelia asked me about it some time later. She seemed genuinely upset.

"What does that mean?" she demanded. "What can it mean?"

"I don't really know. I think that when there are different possibilities for something happening, and normal people believe that one of the possibilities occurs and the others don't, these people believe that they all happen, except that they all happen in different universes, so we don't know that they're happening. Something like that. Don't quote me on it."

"That's insane. Why do they believe it?"

"I'm not sure. I think they need it for their equations to come out right. You know, on a subatomic level."

"Maybe their equations are wrong."

"They don't believe that's possible."

"So there are thousands of universes with no Cornelia? And hundreds of other versions of Cornelia as well? You don't believe that, do you?"

"No, no, of course not. I'm not sure anyone really believes it. They just use it for stories, like they do time travel and zombies. You know, as a plotline for movies and TV shows and paperbacks. Maybe it's only the real smart ones, the ones that understand the equations, who actually believe it."

"I'm glad I'm dumb."

"Me too."

That conversation took place later and elsewhere. On St. John the Baptist's Day, no one was worrying about what the folks were doing in the other universes. Cornelia and I soon found ourselves impressed into bringing big bowls of fruit around for the guests. Still no one asked who I was. The Geese assumed I was a Dragon and the Dragons had gotten used to me. After the fruit, there came the dark wine brought in many glasses on silver trays. They did not trust me with that, wisely. It was circulated by Cornelia and the ex-con, the former "Army Jerry" who had come down into the basement months before and who had pegged me as a Bellyman. He moved surely up and downstairs, and between guests. Cornelia performed a more theatrical balancing act, but the job still got done. In no time we were all standing with goblets of red wine in our hands.

"Toast!" Balin gave a sharp shout that arrested the attention of the revelers.

His brother finished.

"To the King who was, to the Queen who is, and to the King who will be again."

There was a fierce cheer and we all tipped our glasses and drank deep. Someone began singing, and they all joined in.

Chevaliers de la Table Ronde
Goûtons voir si le vin est bon
Chevaliers de la Table Ronde
Goûtons voir si le vin est bon
Goûtons voir oui oui oui
Goûtons voir non non non...

I didn't know good wine from bad, this being my first glass, but it certainly did grow on me. It had a lovely fragrance as well. I soon had a full glass again, filled by someone unnoticed as I watched Miss Widdershins singing at the top of the stairs. It was a long song. Someone tugged my sleeve.

"Come on," said Cornelia. "I'll show you where the best fruit is."

In the narrow plot across the driveway someone had planted strawberries.

"There aren't near enough for the company, but there are enough for us," said Cornelia.

We pushed the big flat dark green leaves aside and hunted for the berries, pinching them off the woody stems where we found them. Soon we each had a couple of handfuls.

"Let's have a reverse picnic. I used to do this when I was a little girl."

She led me into the house. We had to put our wine glasses down on the gravel of the driveway and make two trips. Soon we were seated on the floor underneath the dining room table, with the chairs hemming us in on all sides. Cornelia pulled the last chair in behind her, as if she were closing the door of a cave. We ate the strawberries off the floor. They were smaller than store-bought but the flavor was intense, as heady as the wine.

"I used to do this when I was little. I'd sit under the kitchen table in our trailer and have picnics and tea parties with my stuffed animals. No one else could fit. My mother and father would sit up top and pass down tea and cake to me."

She started telling me about growing up with the Cats, reminiscing as if she were an old lady and her childhood a distant memory. I got the impression of muddy lanes and open fires and people moving in and out. There was a lot of music and dancing. Cornelia spoke of Mary, the young woman I had seen hurrying to the gathering.

"She could do the same steps as everyone else, but there was a certain way she held her head." Cornelia tried to demonstrate under the table. "She made everyone else want to dance and everyone else think that they could."

All at once she fell silent, and I could see the effort of listening written on her face. She held a finger to her lips. We heard the boards creak and then voices sound clear above us, as several people walked into the room.

"It seems that it would be safest and simplest to move it," said Emile Stokowsky. "It is small enough that it could be removed without anyone noticing."

"We have adequate security," replied Miss Widdershins.

"I don't think you appreciate the worth of the painting. I mean monetarily. The man has only thirty-five authenticated works extant. Thirty-five in the whole world! By way of comparison, there was a Van Gogh sold recently for eighty two million dollars. It was a portrait, and there are two versions extant of that work alone. Two versions of that single work and one sold for eighty two million."

"Can we assume it was at least the better of the two versions?" said Thomas the Rhymer.

One of the chairs tipped away slightly, as someone put a hand on the back. Cornelia and I stared at one another. If they sat at the table, the chances were high that we would be kicked and discovered.

"We have it guarded."

"Of course, and our adversaries have no doubt noticed that and marked the guards, their numbers, their comings and goings. For the amount of money we are talking about I fear that they would make an attempt with MP-5s or what have you. It is not safe. You are not safe."

"But if we move it and they don't know we've moved it, how would that lessen the chance of an assault?" asked Thomas.

"This is true. Perhaps something could be done with decoys. Let them see us move a number of false paintings out."

"Decoys, I like," said Miss Widdershins. "But the painting stays with me, with the Pendragon, as it has for four hundred years."

The chair tipped back down.

"If they did shoot their way in and kill the lot of us," asked Thomas, "How could they sell it?"

"Private collector, perhaps. But remember, there would be nothing to say the picture had ever been here. We would not tell. It would be child's play to develop a provenance, bribe a few experts. You know as well as I, better perhaps, how much is currently in museums that was stolen from its rightful owners at one time or another. They could say it went missing in the Second World War. People are always claiming restitution for what was never theirs in the first place. Or go back further, to the Napoleonic Wars. For a hundred million, for two hundred million, these things could be arranged."

"Hmmph. You make good points. And they know we're aware of them and providing against them. Good points," said Miss Widdershins. "It may be time to move soon. But first we settle with Gone-Away."

"Understood."

We listened to their footsteps as they moved away.

3.

In due time we emerged from under the table and made our cautious way out the front door. Cornelia's hat had been knocked off the top of her head, and it clung to her hair at an angle that made her look scandalously tipsy, although she was not. We rejoined the revelers in the back yard. We had both left our wine glasses under the table, along with the caps of numerous strawberries.

"I'll get them later," Cornelia assured me.

It was a day for wine. I was lucky that I had left my glass behind or it would certainly have been refilled, with consequences that could only be unfortunate. The singing continued; French seemed to be the order of the day. They had brought out a carved and cushioned chair for Miss Widdershins and she sat above them all on the landing, spinning the stem of a glass. Thomas the Rhymer stood by her side and some of the familiar Dragons festooned the steps at her feet. There were women about the place, all in long dresses despite the heat, but they were far fewer than the men. I suppose that was only natural, since a lot of the men were there as guards.

One of the women reached up and put the cap back atop Cornelia's head, arranging her hair so as to support it in its rightful place. She was short, about Miss Widdershins' height, but thin, with sharp cheekbones and very pale fine red hair pulled straight back. After she had finished, the man who was with her, our old friend from the basement, handed her a slender cigar that she had apparently set aside to assist Cornelia. She had a bit of a tough look about her, like a hardworking waitress approaching middle age.

The grouping by the steps began a new song. The folk in the yard, some of whom had been clearing a space for what looked like a game of *bocce,* all at once stopped their pastime.

Vive le vieux vin de vigne
Le vieux vin Gaulois

The song was known to them. The Dragons joined the chorus. Cornelia, inspired, did a fling. The hat stayed on. She was a good dancer; I knew she would be. It was a fearsome song. As I watched the faces of the singers and the light that shone in their faces, it seemed they had called a fierce and an ancient world with them, and through them, into the little everyday yard. I half expected them to vanish when the song ended, and take me with them.

They did not, and when the song and the cheers had died, the players went back to their game. It was time for me to leave. I said goodbye to Cornelia, and took an appropriately formal leave of my hostess. Cornelia walked me to the end of the block. We didn't talk much about the new developments, we were both still mulling them over. It was the first time that I realized that she might be in some personal danger.

I think I weaved a bit on the way home; it's a difficult judgement to make of yourself. I am sure I had the beginnings of a foolish smile on my face. I had only drunk two full glasses of wine, but I was a lightweight and it was new to me. As it happened, there was no one home so I did not have to make an unaccustomed effort to compose myself. I settled down to a comfortable afternoon nap, and was right as rain, teeth brushed and faced washed, by dinnertime.

When I closed my eyes that night, up in my room alone, I conjured to my mind again the sight and the sound of the Dragons singing their last mad song, while the red wine flowed and Cornelia danced and Queen Vivien presided:

Glaive maître des batailles
Glaive, honneur à toi

12. The Thieves

1.

Dear James,

June 26th
St. Anthelm's Day
(I looked it up)

Please come to the Teach Mór on Saturday morning, say 10 o'clock, or eleven. It's a matter of the gravest importance. Be prepared to travel.

Yours,

Cornelia

I found this missive in the drop box when I chanced to check it Friday morning. It was by sheer luck that I found it; we saw each other so much over the summer that there was no longer much need for letters.

The *"Teach Mór"* was her new name for Miss Widdershins' house. It meant the "Big House," the great lady's stronghold, where money changed hands, and deals were made, and fates were determined.

I was puzzled by the phrase "be prepared to travel." Was I supposed to bring a suitcase and a change of clothes? Was I supposed to arrive unencumbered? Based on our past history, I though the safest thing I could do would be to bring as much money as I could honestly lay my hands on, and little else. I didn't have much of my own, but I borrowed some from my sister, and came up with maybe thirty or forty dollars.

There was a bit of a rigmarole Saturday morning, getting

away and getting free at the appointed time, but my parents were pliable when it came to me spending time with Cornelia. I wonder if they too somehow sensed that it couldn't go on for long. In any case, I made it to the front door within the suggested time frame. Cornelia was waiting for me.

"Just a second."

She ducked back into the house.

"Auntie, I'm going with James now," she called.

She took the steps at one jump.

"Let's go. We can still catch the 10:57 if we hurry. I'll explain when we get to the station."

2.

Cornelia stalked rapidly along the sidewalk, and I hurried to keep up.

"Where are we going?"

"It's a surprise."

"A hint?"

"We're going to the city."

"Any reason?"

"I'll tell you on the train. *Vite, vite! Nous sommes bien pressés.* If we miss this train we'll have to wait an hour."

"Don't worry, we have time."

I knew exactly how long it took to walk to the station, knowledge acquired from hurrying to get to Mets games. I had walked past these lawns, bushes and houses for years. The topography had changed in the last few months. One of the corner houses was gone, and a new brick edifice was going up behind plywood. It was a loss, I thought. The previous owner had been an Italian, and his summertime yard was lush with leafy edibles, cucumbers, eggplants, weird-looking heads of lettuce. I had learned a lot over the years by walking past that house.

"You're very mysterious," I said.

"I like being mysterious."

"Just so as I can find my way home again."

We bought our tickets inside the neat little station house and waited down by the tracks. I always liked looking at the random elements waiting to be carried to Manhattan. I usually tried to guess why they were traveling. I remember there was one little guy in denim jacket and pants, with boots and an instrument case. He had big fluffy hair that reached halfway down his back. I figured him for a rock musician at a bar or club. I am sure he commanded the stage, but on the street he just looked prematurely aged and tired. There was the usual clutch of Chinese girls, nicely dressed. I thought maybe they were going to a Test Prep or music lessons of some sort.

When the train arrived, we found ourselves a couple of free seats facing forward. As soon as we were settled, I turned to Cornelia.

"Well?"

"We're going to see the Art Thief."

"What?"

"My investigations have at last paid off. I found his address on some papers that Auntie had poorly concealed."

"Where?"

The address she gave meant nothing to me. It was not, I later found, in any of the recognized gallery areas of Manhattan. Whether the isolated location meant that the Thief's place was not one of the more prestigious galleries, or whether it was just happenstance, I still do not know. It is my impression that such places are scattered throughout Manhattan.

"Why?"

"Interest. Don't you want to see what he looks like? Maybe he has some of our things on display."

I considered this.

"I don't know if that's such a good idea. What's he gonna think when two kids wander into his store with no hope of buying anything? Isn't he going to wonder what we're doing there?"

She considered that.

"Well, we can at least walk past. Check out the lay of the land. I'm tired of waiting around at home."

I didn't see what good could come of this, but after all, it was her family not mine.

We looked out the window at the back yards speeding past, snapshots of other lives, and then at a wall of compact brick house fronts that faced the train tracks across a long narrow street. At irregular intervals, the barrier would burst open to reveal broad busy neighborhoods, each like the center of its own town, then close up again. As we got closer to the city we passed a collection of narrow cultivated plots tucked behind what looked like a giant warehouse, the work of urban gardeners, cultivated with varying levels of care and skill. Then it was all tracks, a vast aging network with the weeds growing in between, and then we were underground.

In the dark tunnel, while we waited for a train to clear ahead of us, Cornelia said: "We'll just walk past at first. See what kind of a place it is. I would like to get a glimpse of the owner."

"I still don't see what's the purpose."

"I want to see the little man who is trying to destroy us."

After a while I said:

"Suppose we run into one of those watchers? They probably know what we look like. You certainly, me maybe. If they recognize us, they'll know we're on to them."

"Those guys were pulled. They haven't been around for a while." She thought deeper. I could see she was having doubts. "Maybe you're right. We'll just walk past. Take a quick look. Now that we're here, we can at least do that."

The train started again abruptly, and we resumed our silent staring.

When the train stopped and we stepped out onto the platform, it took us a while to get our bearings. The first short staircase only brought us up to the level of the subway. I knew we would not be taking any more trains if the store was within walking distance, and as long as it was in Manhattan, Cornelia would consider it within walking distance. Anyone could see that neither of us was used to the station; we impeded the feverish flow of foot traffic as we stood and looked for signs. I think we both enjoyed the querulous impatience we occasioned in others. They deserved to suffer for their lack of character.

We arose onto Seventh Avenue. The city was a foreign country to me, one that I normally did not enjoy visiting. Today was different; I was with them but not of them. I had my own purpose, one they couldn't hope to understand. It was a city of foreigners, anyway, Bellymen from all over the country and all over the world, strangers passing roughly on the street and all hurrying to dive into their own particular rabbit holes. Watching over it all were the police, more and more with each passing year, and now also, at the top of the stairs, on street level and at more than one junction in the station, there stood at ease men and women in green fatigues, a new paramilitary presence. I took them to be National Guard, but I really didn't know what their purpose was. My father had noted their advent with grim enjoyment. This was before the surveillance cameras started going up all over the city.

We walked south. The crowds were thick, and Cornelia adjusted her pace to a patient amble. The heat wave of the past few days had broken, but it was still a warm summer's day, coarsened by the exhalations of the street, and I was glad to take it easy. There were plenty of interesting shops to look at, as we worked our way south. We stayed on Seventh Avenue a good long while. Too long it turned out; when we made our left turn we found ourselves hung up for a time in short zigzagging streets where it was difficult to gauge the directions of the compass. I was interested to observe the changes in style of person as we traversed various neighborhoods. The intense little NYU students were easy to pick out, practicing moodiness. The foreign tourists, especially the German women with their scrubbed good looks, were the one constant throughout the town, and a welcome, brightening variation against the often glum background.

We passed north of Washington Square, and were soon nearing our destination. There were older buildings here. Moldings appeared along brick walls, false balconies grew under windows, ironwork adorned stairways and entrances. Most of the buildings were unimproved and had a down-at-heel look, but there were also a number of showpieces that were in various stages of renovation.

We had long been walking with one goal in mind, but when we reached our block it seemed sudden to us. We had barely spoken a word since we left the station. Cornelia stopped at the corner and read out the address again to me. We were on the correct side of the street.

"We'll just walk by, at first. Maybe we can look in the window if it seems safe."

"We'll play it by ear," I suggested.

"Inconspicuous, that's the watchword."

We walked slowly down the street, looking at the numbers, like children playing a children's game, ready to run at the first alarm. It was a mixed block, some storefronts, some narrow private entrances. It was an interesting block; there was a foreign bookstore, a poster shop below street level, a place that looked like it sold fancy garden accents with lots of brass pipe sprouting from marble, and then we came to the Thief's place.

He'd created an attractive storefront. A smooth concrete space in front of the shop was marked off by an intricate black iron railing. I wondered if there had originally been a staircase to a lower story, now filled in. The window too was bordered by ironwork, and the name of the shop spelled out in large raised gilded letters laid over a background of thick dull green paint. A variety of items was arranged within the window, which was very subtly tinted to frustrate harmful solar radiation. Despite our previous resolve, Cornelia and I stopped and stared.

"I wonder if any of that stuff is ours," said Cornelia.

With her feet planted on the cement of the sidewalk, she leaned over the railing, folding at the waist. Further and further she bent. It was as if her feet remembered their mission of secrecy, while the rest of her body forgot.

"There, that book. That little prayer book. I think that's ours."

She leaned for a closer look. She started suddenly rotating her outstretched arms backward in rapid circles. She had overbalanced.

"Help! Help!"

I made a grab for her, and reached her just as her feet were leaving the ground. I clutched a big handful of her wiry hair; there was simply nowhere else to hold. We were standing like that, with Cornelia balanced over the railing in a plank position with her arms flailing wildly and me pulling hard with my fist buried in her curls as if I were trying to stop her from taking off, when a bell rang and the proprietor of the store walked out and saw us.

He was clearly the proprietor, with all the complacency of ownership. He was a fat man with a sparse beard. He was dressed casually, without tie or jacket, in a pale grey short-sleeved shirt and jeans, a working shopkeeper despite the pricy merchandise. He regarded the scene before him.

"See anything you like?"

I had at last dragged Cornelia back to the vertical, by getting close and pressing down on her legs.

"Oh, yes, lots," she managed to say in reply.

"You can come around the railing for a closer look."

By this point we had both belatedly recovered our caution.

"Oh, no, we don't have any money for shopping."

"Well, then, you'd better go out and get some," said the man with a laugh, though not unkindly. "But it doesn't cost anything to look in the window."

There was a brief silence.

"You have a … you have an elegant store," said Cornelia at last. "Well, gotta go now."

We went.

3.

Shortly thereafter we sat perched on the edge of a large cement planter that stood near a busy street corner, eating hot dogs and anatomizing our failure in the shade of an ornamental tree.

"Boy, I can't believe that. Everything went wrong."

It was true. Even her speech, her use of the word elegant, would only serve to fix her in the shopkeeper's mind.

She shook her head. We were both ravenous, and after we

finished stuffing the hotdogs, we went back for more. We had somehow found a push cart, although I thought that the mayor had banished them all from the streets. Perhaps the permissions varied by district. I got mustard on my pants, as I always did; Cornelia was neater.

She looked at me.

"Ain't we a pair," she said, ruefully.

"Well, he still doesn't know who we are," I said. "I mean, face it, there's no reason for him to know who we are or to connect us to the Dragons, unless he's seen us before. As far as I know, he hasn't."

"Did he have a camera out front? A lot of places do. Someone might recognize us from the film."

"I didn't notice. Anyway, why would anyone look through hours of surveillance footage because a couple of kids looked in their front window?"

"Yeah, I guess so." She sighed. "I'd make a lousy spy."

"Me too."

"At least you weren't taking a swan dive into his window. By the way, that was our book, I'm sure of it. It's really old. It's hand written, not printed. We picked it up in France, I think in Grenoble. It's a prayer book. I bet it's worth money. That's all they care about."

"He didn't seem like a bad guy," I said reflectively.

"What did you expect, horns? People like that know how to put up a front. But inside? Heart of stone."

We sat enjoying our hot dogs and watching the people, the seemingly inexhaustible stream of people, smart in skirts, easy in pants, sloppy in tank tops, proud in suits. I loved looking at the faces, especially the women, the structure of the faces built around the cheekbones. I could sit for hours. I looked at the girl by my side, as she sat slightly moving to whatever tune she was playing inside her head.

She looked at me.

"I guess we'd better be getting back," she said.

After we dumped our wrappings and leavings in the garbage,

Cornelia said, "Let's walk back on the same block. We can walk on the other side of the street. We'll just pass by."

She certainly is mercurial, I thought.

We retraced our steps until we came to the end of the Thief's block, where we crossed to the other side. We moved slowly and delicately along the sidewalk, trying to look without looking, to see without being seen.

We were getting close when she suddenly grabbed me with both hands and stopped short. I turned to her in surprise and saw her eyes wide open in an almost comic alarm.

"Oh my gosh. That's him. Going into the store now. That's Con Gone-Away! Don't look!"

I looked and saw a man pausing outside the shop, casually looking in the window that had ensnared us just a short time before. He was not at all as I expected. I had assumed a man like the shopkeeper himself, a Bellyman, slack, greedy, perhaps a bit self-indulgent. From where I stood he looked to be pure Dragon, foreign, hard. He took a quick look behind him before he entered, and I saw the same look I had seen in the others, but angry as they were not, or so it seemed to me.

All this I saw and noted in a moment, before he walked into the Thief's lair, and Cornelia pulled me into a waiting alley.

13. The Traitor

We walked a few steps up the alley. Cornelia leaned against the wall farthest from the Thief's shop. It was more of a driveway than an alley, a place for the stores to receive and dispatch deliveries. There were stacks of merchandise at entrances on either side. There was enough room, barely, to accommodate a small truck. Fire escapes climbed the walls like vines. I had a vague impression of shadowed figures in motion further in from the street than we were.

"Wow," said Cornelia. "What luck! But good luck or bad luck?"

"Did he see you?"

"I don't think so. I hope not. Although …"

Here she paused and thought, then thought some more.

"You know, even if he did see me, I don't think he'd recognize me. The last time he saw me, I was six years old. My hair was lighter, and way shorter. I was little and fat."

"You were fat?"

"We'll say 'plumpish.' "

She said again, "I don't think he'd recognize me. In fact I'm sure of it. And he doesn't know you at all. Let's follow him."

"Are you sure that's a good idea? What if he notices us?"

"Faces in the crowd, James, waifs and strays. We'll be careful. If things look dangerous we'll just break it off."

"We don't have a very good record so far."

Without noticing, we had been drifting up the alley as we talked. We were suddenly addressed by a new voice.

"What are you doing here? Huh? What are you kids doing here?"

It was an aggressive voice, needlessly aggressive given the circumstances. We looked up, surprised. We saw a heavy-set man with one of those fashionable little goatees. A web tattoo spread across his neck. He was wearing a dirty tank top and shorts. He had little eyes, nasty little eyes. He had been stacking flat boxes to put in a long lean vintage muscle car. He was close.

"What are you doing?" he asked.

"Mind your business," said Cornelia.

"Mind my business? This is my business. You're on private property."

Someone else darkened the doorway behind him, creating a definite sense of menace. The reaction to our offense was so disproportionate that Cornelia and I were both nonplussed.

For some reason that puzzles me now, I decided to try to channel my inner Rockford.

"We're looking for Taggart Industries," I said. "They make audio components," and I gave him a street address one block over. He wasn't interested.

"What are you talking about? Come here."

The man advanced on me fast.

"Watch it, bub," suggested Cornelia.

The man leered at her.

"Come here, come here," he kept saying and started reaching, but he had trouble deciding which of us he wanted to grab first. The other man came out of the doorway. I thought he looked as surprised as we were by the turn of events. We were both still backing away at this point, so the tattooed man was closing distance. He turned towards Cornelia and had her suddenly backed against the opposite wall. She kept sliding along the wall toward the street. I had actually lifted my leg, preparatory to kicking him behind the knee and hoping for the best, when Cornelia made a quick movement and poked him in the elbow with a knife she had produced with the facility of a magician.

He gave a cry and started back.

"What the …?"

We were down the alley and on the street before he could

finish his sentence. We left the Thief's store behind us and raced, sometimes on the sidewalk, sometimes in the street, until we stood on a corner a block and half away from the alley.

We leaned on our knees, panting and looked back for pursuers. There were none.

"That was the single strangest thing that has ever happened to me," said Cornelia at last.

2.

"*What* was he thinking? What could he have been thinking?"

I had to agree with her. Is this the way it was? Step off the main street for a moment and you find yourself in the jungle? Did all these bright entrances hide dens of madness?

"You people are just weird," said Cornelia.

I thought about it and decided that, given the location and the circumstances, the man probably never intended to do us serious harm, only to scare us. Wasn't he surprised?

"I had to tag him," said Cornelia. "Like Uncle Tom always says, if you need to pull a weapon, you probably need to use it."

"Oh, absolutely."

"Now I have to dump this thing, in case he calls the cops."

Cornelia showed me the handle of the switchblade, already folded in her back pocket.

"In case *he* calls the cops? He was threatening us."

"That's not the way it works, James. If they find you with a concealed weapon, that's all they care about. In New York, possession is nine points of the law. I gotta get rid of this."

She glanced up and down the avenue.

"Look. I'll run up the street and find a place where I can safely dump this. I don't want to lose Gone Away, though. Here's what we do. You go back a block and wait around the corner to see if he comes out. You know: linger. I'll join you as soon as I can."

"Suppose he walks the other direction?"

"You'll be able to see. If he leaves, follow him. We can meet up again at Penn Station. Failing that, we can meet up again at home. But I shouldn't be long."

She ran away north.

As was customary with Cornelia's plans, flaws became apparent to me as I moved to execute this one. If the man actually did call the police, wouldn't they find me as I lingered on the corner? Still, without Cornelia and her blade, what could they pin on me? Suppose the tank-top man himself walked by as I was waiting? Or, worse, drove by? Suppose I followed Con Gone-Away and he took a train to New Jersey? Suppose I ran out of money? I would just have to break off pursuit before that happened.

Lingering proved difficult. It was a nothing corner. There was no reason for anyone to spend any time there. I decided to pretend I was waiting for someone. I periodically walked to the curb and anxiously looked up and down the avenue. I had been enacting that simple deception for less than fifteen minutes when I saw Con Gone-Away crossing the avenue on the other side of the street, heading west. I let him cross over, then began my pursuit.

My only concern now was that I not be detected. The more I saw of this man the less I liked him. He was a housewrecker and I had no intention of getting within arm's reach of him. He was a little over medium height, and wide. His shoulders tormented the tan leather jacket he was wearing. He moved with aggression. People avoided him on the sidewalk.

I had to hurry to keep up. I kept to the other, the south side of the street, dodging around the opposing foot traffic. It soon became clear that there was little need for caution. He was single-minded and looked neither right nor left.

In time, he turned north, and thereafter I found myself on the same side of the street as I followed him. I had no idea how far he would walk. Once I was caught standing in a crowd with him, waiting for the light to change, but there was nothing about me to attract anyone's attention. Always I tried to let him get ahead of me, but I had to make sure I wasn't caught on the wrong side of the light when it changed.

I didn't know the geography of Manhattan, so it was a surprise to me to see Union Square Park ahead of me, as I crossed 14th

Street at a safe distance from my quarry. Halfway across the road, I felt a tug at my sleeve and a familiar presence close by my side.

"I've been following you for blocks. Where is he? I don't see him."

"Right there." I pointed from the hip. "I think he's about to go down into the subway."

We followed him into the hole. Before we went underground I had a brief sense of the park and of all the busy Bellymen at their various forms of recreation. If things had been different, I would have liked to stay for a while.

We almost lost him in the subway. Neither Cornelia nor I had a Metro Card, and she was positively hopping up and down in frustration as we waited in the short line and as the token booth clerk and I tried to reach a mutual understanding. We had to pop our heads up and check a number of tracks until we saw him waiting for the northbound express, and it was only by taking the stairs at a dead run, both down and up, that we were able to board his train before the doors closed.

As it happened, he got off at the first stop, 34th street. When we looked out of our car, we saw him already with a foot on the stairs. The noisy urban canyon above the tracks was thronged with people, but our man was easy to follow. If he had turned around once at this point, he might have noticed us, since after our mad dash in the subway we had more or less thrown caution to the wind. He did not turn around, however, and I think by this time we both knew where he was going.

We followed him back down into Penn Station, past the paramilitaries, past the police, past a saxophone wailing over an open case, all the way back to the Long Island Railroad terminal. We watched him scanning the big board for the time of his train.

"What do you think?" asked Cornelia.

"Queens, I bet. Port Washington branch. I keep my friends close and my enemies closer."

There was no way to tell which was his line. He did not buy a ticket, only walked to look at one of the flip boards, as it announced the track of each train in turn. Scores, maybe hundreds of people stood in a loose crowd, gazing intently at the boards. When a new track number appeared, the crowd suddenly thinned, as the particles of humanity detached themselves and headed for the proper staircase, where they squeezed through the door then filed below like grains of sand through an hourglass. He watched the board; we watched him.

When the moment came, he went where we thought he would, down the stairs to the Port Washington train. It was difficult to follow him in the crush. Even Cornelia and I were separated for a while. We hadn't learned the moves, how to insinuate our bodies through the shifting human maze without causing offense or injury. Cornelia kept contact with him, and I kept my eyes on her great mass of hair, so we followed him down the platform and into his car.

He sat with his back to the door. The trains had two corrals of seats adjacent to each door, each corral consisting of five seats facing each other, three on one side and two on the other. He sat in the corner against the wall, on the innermost of the two seats. We moved down the car and picked a bench across the aisle, from which we could see if he rose to leave. He pulled out a fat paperback, which seemed like an incongruously innocent pastime for so desperate a villain. When the train started and the conductor passed, Gone Away showed a monthly ticket without looking up.

Cornelia and I made a bet as to where he'd get off. She thought it would be after our stop; I picked before, to make things interesting. The trains on the weekend were all locals, so we were sure to make every stop. This was the most dangerous part yet of our surveillance, sitting facing him across the train. If he looked up and saw us staring, he could not help but mark the intensity of our interest. We forced ourselves to spend most of our time looking resolutely out the window. I don't think I noticed anything, except sometimes the birds flashing past the window or hopping after crumbs on the platforms.

I lost my bet. When the doors opened and closed for our stop, he still had not moved. The train picked up speed again, and the windows showed us the bay and the salt flats where Cornelia and I had gone walking that first day I learned about the tribes. After the close city I was grateful for a glimpse of the wide spaces.

Cornelia poked me in the arm. Gone Away had risen and was standing by the door.

"So close," she whispered.

No one else was standing. We let him walk out the door before we rose. Fortunately, when we got out on the platform there were other folk who had disembarked from other cars, so we were able to fall in at the rear of the line. We could see Gone Way toward the head of the line. He rocked back and forth in a peculiar nautical motion as he took the steps.

There were a lot of hills on this side of the bay. It was an old and a wealthy area, where the crooked streets wound among big old houses. Our path took us mostly uphill. The crowd thinned out quickly and soon we were the only walkers, following Con Gone Away at a good distance, falling farther and farther behind for safety's sake. After a short time he made a sharp left and disappeared from view. We picked up our pace, but when we got to the corner where he'd turned, he was nowhere to be seen.

We stood for a moment looking up the street. There were only one or two houses on either side that he could have had time to enter before we had reached the corner. It was a long street terminating in a chain-link fence. There was no egress. Beyond the fence lay the tracks of the Long Island Railroad. It was a quiet street. Too quiet, I thought.

"Close enough," said Cornelia. "Let's keep going."

We kept along our way, walking mostly in the street since in many places there were no sidewalks. Finding our way back to the main avenue, we passed a churchyard with many gravestones, some cut sharp, some blurred illegible by age. The church was white with big unstained windows; you could see clear through it. We turned around and looked behind us many times, newly conscious that we too might be followed.

At length we stood on the big busy boulevard. It was the only way back to our houses, and we still had a long walk ahead of us.

"We know where he is now if we need him," said Cornelia. "More or less."

3.

At first Cornelia kept looking behind her, but as we moved farther west along the boulevard, she relaxed. She began swinging her arms as if she were loosening up for exercise, then grabbed my hand and started swinging my arm too. When she left off, she said, "Some nice house he must live in. He must have sold some good stuff already."

"Crime pays."

"For now. If he's so close, I wonder why we haven't just gone out and gotten him by now. It must be the book. He's got something we want, and we've got something he wants. It's a stalemate."

"Would he sell the book?"

"If he did that, he'd be dead for sure. Anyway, I don't know if anyone would want to buy it."

She stopped short for a moment.

"I suppose he could sell parts of it. He could break it up and sell parts of it. I know there are some things he could sell. There's a version in it of the Cattle Raid of Coolinge that's much better than any other version. Maybe he could sell that to a publisher?"

"Maybe a university."

"If he broke it up, there are pieces he could sell."

"And he could keep the pieces he needs for insurance."

We started walking again.

"Would he do that?" she asked.

I couldn't answer. All I could say was, "I'm pretty sure it would lose a lot of value if he broke it up. He probably would only do that as a last resort."

"Let's hope so."

We were passing a driving range, where a long row of golfers whacked little white balls various distances out into a vast green field. The balls sat there in the grass like mushrooms until someone drove by in a cart and scooped them up. We left the sidewalk and walked into the circular gravel driveway so Cornelia could get a better look. She watched the golfers, I watched the people arriving, walking from their cars to the clubhouse with their equipment slung over their shoulders. They looked very serious and very happy. It was a combination I have always liked. This was about the time when the big demographic shift in Queens was becoming obvious; most of the drivers were Asian.

When Cornelia finally tired of the spectacle and we started to leave, I became conscious of the wheels of a car very slowly grinding down the gravel behind us. There were always cars entering and leaving, so we edged over to give it room and thought no more about it.

We had only walked a dozen yards or so away from the driving range, when the car pulled rapidly out of the driveway and came to a stop in the road a few feet ahead of us. We both froze. The driver reached across and rolled the passenger-side window down.

"Get in," he said.

To my surprise, Cornelia ran forward and opened the rear door.

"It's OK," she said to me.

I followed and looked in the car as she slid over, and found myself looking at the former "Army Jerry" who regarded me with an inscrutable expression. He waited until I was inside with the door closed behind me, then turned his attention to pulling out from the curb.

"Cornelia, Cornelia," he said without taking his eyes off the mirrors and the road, "What are we going to do with you?"

Cornelia sat demurely and said nothing. Of course, I thought, with the tribes watching the two thieves, it was no surprise that they would pick us up as well.

"What are you thinking?"

"I was curious. He didn't see us."

"You don't think so? Are you sure about that?"

"Yes."

"He's not a dummy, you know."

"He didn't turn around once."

"Was anyone with him? Are you sure? They are playing for millions here. You don't know how many people are involved. Were you followed yourselves?"

I started noticing that the man was taking an extremely roundabout way back to the big house. The seat cushions sagged and squeaked as we bounced up, down and around the narrow streets. It was another old car. An old Dodge Dart. They didn't let things go to waste.

"I don't think so."

"Yet here I am. There's too much going on here, Cornelia. People watching people, and no one sure of what the other knows. Stay clear of it. We don't need complications."

We were almost back to my house before he addressed me through the rearview mirror.

"I'll drop you off first. It may be a while before you get to see Cornelia again. There's no way around that. But time passes."

He stopped in the middle of the street in front of my house. Before I got out, Cornelia gave my hand a squeeze and twisted her mouth into a wry expression. I stood in the street and watched the car until it turned out of sight.

14. The Reunion

1.

It was a week before I received Cornelia's next letter, though it had been posted earlier. We had gone up to the Catskills for a brief vacation, taking advantage of the Fourth of July holiday. We used to go up to Palenville in the German Catskills; it had been a tradition in my family for seventy years. My grandfather often spoke of one particular swimming hole, of climbing down the rocks into Kaaterskill Creek and paddling and turning in the cold waters fresh off the mountains, of sitting up against the current in a natural stone chair and letting the water flow over and around him. It was right in the middle of town, but sheltered from the view of the uninitiate, a summer paradise for three generations of Wards. It was inaccessible now, closed off behind private property signs. In my time, we drove up to North-South Lake, a pair of lakes set high and flat among the steep little mountains, with sandy beaches and perfect views both short and long, and we swam, and canoed, and ate cheese sandwiches, then stopped at the ice cream place on the way back down through the woods.

Our timing was poor that year for a number of reasons. The Fourth of July fell on a Friday, and the motel we were staying at – usually an idyllic spot with a pure blue deserted swimming pool laid out for our private enjoyment – was suddenly thronged by uncouth revelers barely out of their teens. The last couple of nights were not good. At the same time, the weather, which had been ideal at first, turned nasty, and we drove back through brown air to the sweaty city right in the middle of a heat wave.

I was surprised to see a letter from Cornelia waiting for me. I thought Miss Widdershins might have cut us off entirely.

Dear James, 　　　　　　　　*July 1*
　　　　　　　　　　　　　　St. Oliver Plunkett's Day

　　*I am writing this letter with the full knowledge and per-
mission of Aunt Vivien, although the contents is entirely my
own.*

　　*Well, things went better than they might have. I had to
tell Aunt Vivien everything. Mattheus* [that must have been
the former Army Jerry] *just set me down in front of her and
let me do the talking. We sat at the big table and she sat leaning on her elbow with one finger pressed against her cheek.
I could hear the rings on her other hand tapping on the table
as she listened. She looked at me and let me stumble through
the whole story without saying a word. Then I was really surprised. She just told me to go up to my room in a real quiet
voice. A little while later she came up and sat next to me on
the bed amongst my stuffed animals and explained all the
reasons why I shouldn't have done what I did. She explained
it like a duel. She says that if he knows where we are and we
know where he is, and if he knows what we have and we know
what he has, then we are both in measure. We are both trying
to steal measure on the other. If we get careless and make a
mistake, for instance, if we spook him and he takes off and we
no longer know where he is, then we lose measure and that's
when we get touched. It made sense to me.* [It didn't to me,
exactly.] *She also said that he might have grabbed us and
taken us as hostages, which didn't occur to me.* [Nor to me.]
*I guess it was a pretty dumb thing to do. Well, I never said I
was smart. So anyway, we have to cut all that out.*

　　*She didn't forbid me to see you or to leave the house or
anything, but I think it would probably be a good idea for us
not to go over each other's houses for a while.*

　　*One thing was kind of funny. She was explaining to me
that I wasn't a child any more, that I was a young lady and I
had to start thinking like one and taking responsibility, and
the whole time she was talking she had my big stuffed rabbit*

sitting in her lap and she was kind of absent-mindedly pat-ting it on the head and playing with its ears. I thought it was pretty funny, but I didn't smile.

See you in a while,

Cornelia

P.S. I hope you had a nice vacation.

I agreed with Cornelia; I thought things had gone much better than they might have gone. With the memory of Cornelia's week-long sentence after our May Day escapade, I had been afraid of a month's separation at the least. It seemed that Miss Widdershins had decided to take a different tack, putting Cornelia on her honor. Still, I didn't think it prudent to show my face at the house for a while.

There was plenty at home to keep me busy. All sorts of un-pleasant weeds were making their presence felt, and had to be dealt with in our customary unsystematic way as soon as the heat wave broke. We also spent some time clearing old junk out of the basement and bringing new junk down. My grandfather took the lead in this; he always felt peppier after our Catskill vacations. The swimming never failed to revive him. These were the days he made resolutions, when he believed he could put the clock back to a time when he could walk and move and rise and sit freely.

"I must remember to walk when the weather is good," he said. "Take advantage of the days I have."

I was always ready to walk with him.

2.

*T*he first Friday after our vacation saw my grandfather and me in the park on a late morning ramble. We began with our usual circuit around the ball fields, walking in the opposite of our usu-al direction for some reason. The fields were deserted except for one determined high school kid running patterns across the grass while his father or uncle or coach rifled the ball to him over and again. No matter the season, this one was faithful to football, his true love.

As we passed them, I was conscious of a high distant sound calling faintly from somewhere up the slope. I thought at first that I might have been imagining it, but as we swung east around the field it got clearer, now with a bass blended in, until even my grandfather could hear it. We found a solitary piper pacing in the shadow of the tangled row of trees on the edge of the park. He was playing with his head inclined toward his drones, and at intervals he would leave off the chanter and reach up to twist the bass drone or one of the tenors. Then he'd rattle off a quick tuning phrase and try out another longer tune. The great highland bagpipe has a reputation as a loud and a blaring instrument, but here in the outdoors, where it was meant to be played, and against the background dull roar of the city, the pipes sounded smooth and precise and remarkably sweet. My grandfather listened with a faint smile on his face, and his stick clasped behind his back, and I listened with him, as the piper alternated between the playing and the tuning. When we turned to leave my grandfather nodded to the piper, and received a nod of acknowledgement in return.

We walked by a sturdy brick blockhouse that contained restrooms, both gentlemen's and ladies', and an equipment room for the Parks Department. In the seventies, as my father tells me, the restrooms were always locked, ladies and gentlemen being apparently in short supply at the time, but by my time they were generally open again. Our route took us past the blockhouse toward the back of the park, overlooking the bay. I always liked this section; it was like a country lane, or as close to one as I could expect to find, running between two stands of trees. I liked the way the sun would light the grass between the trees, changeable depending on the time of day and the season and the weather.

We were just entering this area, preparing to make a turn, when a little hoop suddenly came hopping up the grass and then rolling along the concrete path right to my grandfather's feet, where it stopped, turned on its axis, leaned and fell.

"What's this?" he asked, pleasantly.

It looked like something from one of those old children's stick-and-hoop games, only smaller.

I would have let it lie, but he stooped and picked it up, just in time for a small red-haired woman in a long pleated dress to make her appearance. She was obviously in quest of the ring. I recognized her from St. John the Baptist's Day. She was the woman who had fixed the hat in Cornelia's hair.

"Is this yours?" asked my grandfather.

"Oh, thank you. Bad throw." She took the ring. "Hello there," she nodded to me, and bounced off over the grass.

By the time we stepped into the clearing, our advent had already been prepared. There was a merry company gathered. Miss Widdershins was sitting on a fine chair under a sort of makeshift pavilion. It was four posts stuck in the grass, with guy wires holding them in place, and a blue and white striped, silver-fringed fabric stretched over the top to keep off the sun. There was even a pennon stirring lazily from a high pole. The red-haired woman was standing alongside Miss Widdershins. The usual crowd was scattered about, most engaged in tossing the ring at a series of short stakes hammered into the earth, a sort of variant of horseshoes, with maybe a little Ultimate Frisbee thrown in. Around the pavilion all eyes were turned towards us in expectation. The players hadn't received the news and were still engrossed in their sport.

My grandfather took in the scene.

"Well," he said. "Look at this."

Cornelia saw us, lightly tossed her ring on the appropriate stake, and came running over the unmowed grass. She, too, was wearing a dress, dark blue, with a longish skirt and short sleeves. Her hair had been arranged in some way, with slender braids circling her head and somewhat directing the usual wild mass into more regular pathways.

"James. Fancy this! Hi, Mr. Ward."

"Hello, Cornelia," said my grandfather. "Is this your family?

I've never met them."

That was about to change, because Miss Widdershins had ris-
en and was floating over the green sea toward us. My grandfather
watched her draw near. She was quite a sight, in billowing white
skirt and flowered bodice, looking like a fairy godmother come to
grant wishes. She was unobtrusively attended at a distance by the
twins, who had detached themselves from their separate games.

"Hello, Mr. Ward." She gave him her hand. "I am Vivien
Widdershins, Cornelia's aunt. You have been kind enough to lend
James to us on many occasions over the last few months. I have
heard a great deal about you. I am so glad to meet you at last."

My grandfather stared at Miss Widdershins in a way that at
first embarrassed me.

"I'm glad to meet you," he responded at last. "It has been a
delight borrowing Cornelia as well."

He looked at her some more, as she waited patiently. Then a
strange expression came over his face, almost cunning, as he half
closed one eye and cocked his head.

"I'm not sure," he said slowly, "but I think I may have met
your father once. No, it would have been your grandfather, fifty
years ago. Is that possible?"

"Quite possible," said Miss Widdershins. "In fact, I am almost
sure of it."

"Come on," said Cornelia to me, pulling me aside. "Let 'em
talk."

I walked into the long weed-tangled grass with Cornelia, then
looked back. Miss Widdershins and my grandfather had linked
arms, and were walking with stately pace along the path, deep in
conversation.

"What's that all about?" I asked Cornelia.

"Reminiscences," said Cornelia, rolling her R. "Nostalgia.
What we do best."

"Cornelia!"

The red-haired woman had returned to the game, and was
tossing a ring up in the air and catching it.

"Play some more?" she said.

"Do you want to play a bit?" Cornelia asked me.

"What are the rules?"

"Easiest thing in the world. Toss the ring over the stakes. If you miss, play it where it lies."

"Your grandfather saved me," explained the red-haired woman.

"Just while they're talking," said Cornelia.

"In or out?" asked the red-haired woman.

"In," said Cornelia and we took our place among the remaining players. We each got our own ring. There was some strategy involved, though not much, since if you tried for a goal from too far a distance and rapped the stake, your ring was liable to bounce off the stake and go rolling. We had only played a few rounds when the programme changed.

A low creak of drones announced the arrival of the piper. Of course, he was one of their party. He took a stand near the pavilion and the people gathered to him. As I joined the throng, I noticed for the first time that Miss Widdershins had a black armband snugly wrapped around her left arm. I drew Cornelia's attention to it.

"Who died?" I asked.

"Arthur, Aunt Vivien's brother. It's the anniversary of his death. It must be thirty years ago now."

"What happened?"

"The doctors killed him. He went to the hospital for something minor and never came out. They made a mistake. It is very sad. He was still a little boy. Every year we mark his death. That's what the piper is doing."

The piper plumped up his bag, and I heard the drones emit a slight groan and the moist air start rushing through the chanter. Then he began to squeeze in earnest, and for a moment, as the three drones growled together before they fell into tune and before the chanter began its song, the pipes sounded truly like the lungs of a great dragon. I have always loved that moment of discordance before the pipes fire up, and I always let mine growl for a while when I get ready to play now, although it is not considered proper form.

It was the saddest tune I have heard. When we heard the piper warming up, he played mostly standards, but this was something different, slow, deliberate, inevitable. It was a proper tribute, grief without sentimentality. It was the *ceol mór* as they say, the big music, and I am fairly sure that the tune he played was "Lament for the Children." He must have been one of the Cats. For a while we listened, but the big music is long music as well, and my grandfather was fading. Miss Widdershins had turned her attention wholly to the piper, so I took a wordless farewell from Cornelia, and we moved slowly away. We rested once on the way back to the parking lot, but the piper was still playing that same tune – I could hear him very faintly – when we got back in the car.

3.

On the way home I asked my grandfather, "What were you and Miss Widdershins talking about? What did you mean when you said you had met her grandfather?"

"A long time ago, before I married your grandmother, she took me over to meet her family. She had a great big extended family. I told you about that. Didn't I tell you about that? It was there I met Vivien Widdershins' grandfather. Your grandmother was especially anxious that I meet him. I guess she wanted his approval. I am sure I told you about that. The girl playing the harp? It must have been the very house you go to visit Cornelia now. How about that?"

"But it's a different house. You pointed out a different house."

"Well, I must have remembered wrong. All those houses look alike to me anyway. It's an easy mistake to make."

As simple as that.

"How did you recognize Miss Widdershins?" I asked. "How did you know she was the other guy's granddaughter?"

"They have kind of a look about them. Or maybe it was more the way people act around them. Or maybe it was just the occasion … it was a similar occasion."

My grandfather had stopped the car by the side of the road,

only a block from our house.

"The old fellow, Miss Widdershins' grandfather, your grandmother called him 'The King.' At first I thought that it was a comical nickname, but she meant it. Your grandmother was kind of a gypsy; I guess they call them Travellers now. But a very special kind. *Sui generis.* I never really got the straight of it; she never told me much. She left all that to marry me. I was always very conscious of what she gave up. She loved her family a great deal."

He paused.

"Of course, her parents were already quite old and she didn't have any brothers or sisters. But there were lots of cousins and aunts and uncles. They would come visit now and again. It was a cousin of hers that gave your father his first violin."

I wanted to ask, "Was she a Dragon? A Goose? A Cat? Something else?" but I didn't think my grandfather would know what I was talking about. So instead I said, "How did Miss Widdershins recognize you?"

"What do you mean? I was with you."

"I mean how did she know that you had met her grandfather fifty years ago?"

"Well," said my grandfather, "I think there's no telling what that woman knows. I mean, she must have known beforehand, mustn't she? She must have known who we were, who you were. I guess they never lost track of us."

I guess not.

When I got home, there was my father on the phone arguing with someone or other, some secularist evangelist preaching the gospel at the last unconverted sinner, and he was saying, "I just don't see what the fascination is. I'd rather look at a puddle. You can get a lot out of a puddle. When I was a kid we used to get those great iridescent rainbow puddles when the rain brought the oil off the street and floated it in the dirty water. Sadly, cars don't leak oil the way they used to. The best puddle I ever saw was at the foot of the Montauk lighthouse. It was a fine sunny day, and down below the lighthouse there was a great big puddle in the sand almost like a lake – you know how clean sand puddles are – and there were swallows flying all across the surface, picking off bugs. I still think of that sometimes …"

My sister was seated at the dining room table eating coconut custard pie.

"Internet again," she explained, jerking her head toward my father. "Did you have a nice walk?"

When my father hung up the phone he said, "I don't know what it is with these people. It's as if they're afraid that if even one person doesn't get with the program and spend every waking moment worshipping technology, the gods of progress will be angered and turn their faces from us and electricity will cease to function."

I thought a lot about my father over the next days. For the first time in my life I felt sorry for him. He was not an unhappy man; in fact, on a personal level he seemed like one of the happiest men I knew. He was content with his life and his family, I thought, but he was at war with everything else. He had been odd man out for so long that he didn't even question it any more. He didn't want what others wanted; he didn't respect what others respected. The world looked one direction, he looked another. It must have been a terrible disadvantage, though, in that perpetual conflict not to know all the reasons. He was betwixt and between, caught between two chairs and sitting in neither.

As for me, I did not feel betrayed or manipulated by either family or friends. I was content to let events unroll as they would. Maybe, in my own way, I felt that I too knew some things that nobody else did. In any case, I was right where I wanted to be. What I felt, most of all, was free.

15. The Judgement

1.

After the friendly meeting in the park between Miss Widdershins and my grandfather, I considered myself dispensed from any obligation to keep my distance from Cornelia and the house. So it was that early next week, rather earlier in the day than was my custom, I found myself walking up Miss Widdershins' front path one more time.

It soon became apparent that something was very wrong. As I approached the steps, a man popped up on the porch from where he had been hiding. I recognized Balin through the screen. When he swung the screen door open, it grated on its hinges. I saw then that the inside front door had been forced and that one of its little windows had been broken. Balin made no comment, only turned his attention back to the street as soon as I passed.

When I entered the house, not without apprehension, I saw Cornelia, in jeans and with a spotted kerchief suppressing her hair, in the act of wringing out a mop in a pail. She saw me, immediately dropped the mop head inside the pail, ran to me and pulled me in with both hands.

"What happened?" I asked.

"They made an attempt," she said. "Early in the morning, just before dawn."

"Are you OK? Is your aunt OK?"

"Both fine."

"What happened? How did it happen?"

Cornelia gazed at me with large mournful eyes. "I slept through it," she said.

"You slept through it? The whole thing?"

"I only awoke when they were carrying the bodies out."

"The bodies?"

"No one was killed, I think. But there was some shooting. Look here."

She drew me to the foot of the stairs and pointed to three holes in the white wall over the landing where the stairs turned to the right.

"And here."

There was a dent and a crack in a heavy brass table lamp alongside the couch close by the stairs.

"Lamp still works." She demonstrated.

"Were any Dragons hurt?"

"Balan was shot. I don't think it's that bad. I hope it isn't. He's being attended to by one of our doctors."

"Anyone else?"

"None of ours. I think some of the Bellymen took it pretty hard, but no one killed. I'm just after mopping up the blood." She pumped the mop up and down in the pail so it looked like a sea creature in an exhibit. "Could you help me pour it out? The bucket is pretty heavy."

I carried the bucket by its handle, while she guided the wooden mop pole around the furniture and out the door. We poured the bucket out in the dirt. It looked like nothing but water curling over the edge. Then we went down to the basement to wash out the mop.

"As far as I can make out, they stormed the house just before dawn. Three men, at least three that we accounted for, maybe four altogether. It wasn't a very good attempt, really. We have men sleeping on the floor, front and back. The guy who came in the back actually stumbled over Balan. Uncle Tom was surprised they didn't do better. See, it's difficult for people to know how many people we really have in here at any one time. Let me show you something."

She balanced the mop upright in the cellar sink and let the water continue flowing over the tentacles. She led me to the back of the cellar. I was astounded to see a hole drilled right through the concrete where the wall met the floor, and a dark tunnel leading away through the earth. It must have been concealed behind the trunks and boxes that now stood on either side.

"The tunnel comes up in the shed." That's what they called the garage. "There's a secret door cut into the back and you can walk right through that into the shed behind it. That one also has a door. They're backed up one against the other so you can pass through easy without being seen unless someone's watching for it and placed just right."

"The house behind you is Dragons too?"

"Yup. Not even the Geese know that. Well, I guess they do now, but they didn't use to."

I bent over and peered into the tunnel. It was big enough to crawl through in relative comfort. It looked old, but it had been reworked carefully and recently, I thought. The floor of the tunnel consisted of fitted bricks, and I could see timber bracing the walls and roof. The breached concrete foundation had been strengthened, effectively I hoped, by a steel beam over the lintel. God knows what it looked like in a hard rain, but maybe they'd accounted for that. They were good workmen.

"Gone Away should have guessed that," said Cornelia thoughtfully. "We always leave an escape hatch, a back way. That's why Uncle Tom thinks that he didn't have anything to do with this. He thinks the Art Thief did it by himself, with his own people. You know, to cut Gone Away out of the deal and get the painting for his own. He really must not have any idea what he's dealing with. Gone Away would carve him up like a Christmas turkey."

"What now?"

We were climbing the steps to the first floor.

"The Geese are going to see to the Art Thief. They're going to warn him off. I think that will be enough, especially when he finds out what happened here. Uncle Tom's already gone out to look up Gone Away. It'll be in the clear light of day, so it's just to talk for now. We think the guys who broke in will keep their mouths shut. Why wouldn't they? They attacked us."

We were seated on the couch now. Cornelia bent towards me.

"The real problem is the neighbors. Did they call the police?

See, the guys used silencers, but even silencers make noise, and there must have been a lot of shouting and wrestling around and screaming. I don't know the blow by blow, but the guys who came in the front went straight for the stairs and tried to shoot their way up. They must have known the painting would be on the second floor, near Auntie's room. Gone Away could have told them that. When I woke up it was all over, including the shouting. Our people were walking, or carrying, the others out and driving them away. Someone might have seen that."

"I was on the second floor looking out the front window watching the figures move across the lawn. It was still dark. Aunt Vivien burst into my room and told me to get ready to move. All through the early morning we were all sitting here on the couch ready to go down the basement and through the tunnel if we had to. That was the worst part. At first we thought for sure someone must have heard something, or seen something. On the other hand, I slept through it. Maybe the neighbors did too? Everyone was trying to be as quiet as possible, both them and us. Anyone who was going to call the cops would have done it by now. So it looks good so far. Now we're just cleaning up the mess, and waiting for the reports to come back."

At that point, I heard the stairs creak, and looked up to see Miss Widdershins and her attendants descending.

2.

Miss Widdershins was dressed in what I took to be a traveling suit, khaki, of a vaguely military appearance, with flaps over numerous pockets. She looked like a woman of the nineteenth century on safari; I was reminded of Deborah Kerr in *King Solomon's Mines*, one of my grandfather's movies. Her hair was pulled back and her blood was up; she looked fierce and ready for action. With her were two soldiers – that is how they seemed to me – whom I didn't know by name but had seen before at odd times and at the gathering on St. John the Baptist's Day. I didn't see Dolores. I assumed she had been bundled through the tunnel to safety when the shooting war started.

Miss Widdershins caught sight of me when she was still on the staircase.

"Well!" she said. "You do keep turning up, don't you?"

Before I could answer she addressed Cornelia.

"Thanks for helping mop up, sweetie. I know it's nasty."

Cornelia shrugged.

"Och, it's not the first time," she said.

Miss Widdershins looked startled.

"Really?"

"No, not really. That was just bravado."

"Well thank you, anyway," said Miss Widdershins with a crooked smile.

They all came down and occupied the various chairs, Miss Widdershins sitting with Cornelia and me on the couch. Balin popped his head in.

"Any word on my brother?"

He looked worried, I would almost say stricken. I wondered how often the two of them had been separated, and found myself flashing back, bizarrely, to Bob and Doug McKenzie in *Strange Brew* when they are separated for the first time in their lives. That was another of my father's "classics"; when his high school friends visited it was only a matter of time before someone got called a "hoser."

"Nothing yet. No news is good news. I'll call you the moment I hear. How does it look outside?"

"Nothing," said Balin. "Nothing and nothing."

She nodded, then turned to me.

"Has Cornelia filled you in?"

"Yes."

"We're under siege conditions until we have reason to think otherwise. Sorry you blundered in, but you'll have to stay a while."

"Can we send him through the tunnel?" asked one of the soldiers, a rangy, vague-looking fellow, like a part-time day laborer.

"No, this house might still be under observation. He came in through the front door, so he's got to leave through the front door.

If they're watching his house too I don't want them to see him come home without knowing how he left here."

That was my first inkling that my own household might not be under immunity.

"Don't worry," said Miss Widdershins, addressing me again. "They're perfectly safe."

"Sorry for causing any trouble," I said.

"No trouble to us."

"The more the merrier," added Cornelia.

"We've got men out, gathering intelligence. We'll let you go as soon as we can. In the meantime, let's all try to relax."

She pulled from one of her pockets a thin elegant brown cigar on a holder. The rangy soldier struck a match, leaned far out of his chair, and lit Miss Widdershins' cigar. When she got it started she settled back on the couch, crossed her legs and puffed in silence. It must have been a rare indulgence, for the house had never before smelled of tobacco smoke, except on the screened porch where the twins held sway.

"Smoke 'em if you got 'em," said the other soldier, a small active-looking man. When he opened his coat to retrieve his pipe, I saw the black butt of an automatic angled down, sticking out of a complicated holster under his left arm.

They smoked for a while in perfect silence. I looked around at the room and saw that already some of the furnishings were disappearing. The vellum books were gone from the little book case. The silver candlesticks were gone as well. They couldn't have removed them all since the morning.

"Do you want to play cards?" asked Cornelia. "In the dining room, away from the smoke stacks."

We sat at the dining room table, towards the back of the house. Cornelia went to get a deck out of the kitchen drawer. I heard her passing a few quiet words with someone. We played Gin Rummy; Cornelia kept score. It was fun at first, but after a while we got tired.

"Chess?"

"Sure."

Cornelia went down to the basement to get a chess set. While she was away, I thought about my family. Were they in danger? For a hundred million dollars and more, dishonest men might take it into their heads to do many extravagant things. If they thought we were important to the Dragons, they might take some of us hostage. My grandfather was home by himself that day. The two of us had been left to fend for ourselves for a few days, as my parents and sister were making a swing through New England, looking through colleges with good music programs. Miss Widdershins had assured me that my household was safe. Maybe the Dragons were watching over our house. I decided to trust her. What else could I do?

Cornelia came back with a more modest chess set than the one we had used in the past, with plastic pieces and a game board of folded cardboard. We played unusually well, taking the opportunity to lose ourselves in the game for a while. We split four games. Eventually this recreation too failed us.

"I wish we could go out," said Cornelia.

We heard a bit of a commotion on the porch, the sound of feet entering the front room, and then low voices. We rose from the table and hurried to peer in at the door. There were a couple of men making a report. One of them I recognized as the singer on the truck bed, from the day when the Dragons fixed up their house and garden and we went to visit our estate. The other was a much younger man, whom I had never seen before. He looked like he needed sleep, like a college kid after an all-nighter.

"They've all been put to bed," the singer was saying. "It has been explained to them in words they can understand. They were hired help anyway."

"Any dead?"

"*Hulla beo*," replied the man, who had seen us standing in the doorway, and had switched to their pidgin.

"All alive," replied Miss Widdershins. "Good."

Cornelia and I went back to the table. Miss Widdershins shortly joined us. She slid a cell phone across the table towards me.

"Call your parents," she said. "Let them know you'll be here for a while. Tell them something."

I went into the kitchen for privacy. There was a guard sitting by the back door, drinking beer in a kitchen chair, with a shotgun within arm's reach lying across the counter. He nodded to me in a distant but courteous manner.

When I got my grandfather on the phone, he was surprised that I was not in the house. He was a late riser in those days.

"I thought you were in your room," he said.

I don't know what I told him. I told him something. I said I was with Cornelia and Aunt Vivien, and we were doing something or going somewhere.

"Take care," he said, as he hung up. I couldn't tell if he was worried.

When I came back to the dining room table, Cornelia turned a happy face towards me.

"Balan's going to be OK," she said. "He's …"

"Stable," supplied her aunt.

Time passed slowly. Miss Widdershins and Cornelia cooked up a great number of bratwurst for us all, which we ate with rye bread and brown mustard. We all drank beer out of brown bottles. We ate in shifts. I went and sat down on the couch, while the folk still in the dining room started up a song. I fell asleep.

When I opened my eyes, I saw Miss Widdershins gazing steadily at me from the easy chair, looking as if she had just awakened herself. The college kid was asleep on the other side of the couch.

"What time is it?" I asked.

"Almost four," she said.

"How long have I been asleep?"

"A good long time. There's nothing as tiring as waiting. I don't want to let you go until we hear from the Geese. They're taking the Devil's own time getting back to us. Cornelia's in the basement."

I went downstairs and found a group of them pitching pennies. I joined them. When a penny bounced wrong and rolled into the far distances, Cornelia and I would race to retrieve it, dodging around the few remaining trunks and cartons. It was a good way to wake up.

There was a shift change. Balin came down and produced an old pink Spalding which he bounced against the wall. The new game was Chinese handball. Crouched alongside him and the others, waiting to take my shots, I felt for the first time keenly what a powerful presence he was. Fast, hard, enduring, physically cunning, unwashed, without any mark of tenderness to himself – he was a brute, he and his brother, a strong wall of defense against anyone who would harm the kingdom.

There were six of us, maybe seven, scuffling around. We had only played a few rounds, before someone opened the door from the kitchen, stuck his head into the cellar, and uttered one word: "Geese!"

We made for the stairs. Cornelia and I were trapped at the back of the pack, moving slowly upward and onward through the bottlenecks on the stairs and at the kitchen door, looking at shoulders and the backs of heads all the way. When we moved into the dining room and got a clear line of sight, we saw our old friend Walsh standing before a seated Miss Widdershins, surrounded by a crowd of eager onlookers.

I recognized most of the faces in the room, even the Geese. I kept seeing the same faces over and over again. Even now, the man with Walsh was one of the mustachioed long-hairs that had been with him at the gathering. I wondered at the time if there were so few left of the tribes, but I have since concluded that I spent most of my time with a sort of small military caste that attended the leaders.

"I actually felt sorry for the poor bastard," Walsh was saying with a somewhat rueful smile. "We put a bag over his head and talked to him in a van. We drove him around while I explained the situation. I drove the visions of Vermeer clear out of his head."

"You're sure about that?"

"Positive. He's a dealer, a merchant, a buyer, a seller, '*ag díol is ag ceannacht,*' not one for the trenches. He thought he saw a chance for easy money and he had to take it. We left him off by the East River. I thought it provided just the right ambience, a nice cautionary reminder. He was only a few blocks from his store, but I don't think he knew where he was."

"Well, that sounds very satisfactory," said Miss Widdershins.

"Oh, one other thing. I hope this is not a problem. I didn't press him on the articles he had already taken. I let him keep it all. Like I said, I hope that's not a problem. It's your stuff, and I know you might want it back."

Miss Widdershins waved her hand.

"A mere *bagatelle*," she said. "A cheap price to pay for peace."

Walsh looked relieved.

"Did you get the impression that Con Cróga was party to the affair?"

"Negative. I don't see any way."

"That was our impression as well. So Con is on his own now."

"What's the story with the shooters, the guys who showed up at the house?"

"Hired help," said Miss Widdershins. "We set them on the straight and narrow, a little the worse for wear. None dead."

"Excellent."

"Please convey my thanks and my compliments to Colonel MacOwen. Tell him we'll settle with Con. We're just waiting for Tommy to come back. Well, this calls for a celebratory drink, I think. Ah, there you are," for the college kid had already brought out a fat full bottle of whiskey and a couple of glasses. Miss Widdershins and Walsh drank from the glasses, the others all took swigs out of the bottle and from the other bottles that crossed the room from hand to hand, following various paths. I had the sense to let them pass untasted.

3.

Cornelia and I sat at the dining room table, as the crowd in the front room gradually thinned out.

"Here's how *we* celebrate," she said.

She brought in an extra large, extra thick chocolate bar, which we broke up and ate slowly and methodically, square by square. We didn't speak much, but listened to the ebb of conversation in the rest of the house.

After a while, Miss Widdershins walked in and told me:

"It's safe to go home now. Con Cróga wouldn't bother your family, and all the *Fir Bullug* have been pacified. But I'm not putting you out," she hastened to add, "stay as long as you like."

I stayed until Cornelia and I finished the chocolate and for a time afterwards, as we sat quiet, blinking, and dazed. The sun was moving toward its setting and the light in the dining room was muted and golden, more delicious even than the chocolate. When the time came, I rose to go.

Before I could reach the front door, it opened and Thomas stepped in, and he had returned with a message from Con Gone Away. We stepped back to let him pass. The attention of everyone in the room was fixed on him as he walked up to Miss Widdershins. Even in this company of hard men, it was easily seen that the champion had arrived.

Miss Widdershins rose from her chair.

"I've spoken with Con Cróga," he said.

"Yes?"

He bent forward and whispered something in her ear.

"A moment, please," she said to the company and they began to ascend the stairs together.

I couldn't have left at that point even if I'd wanted to, for Cornelia had hooked a finger through my belt loop and was holding me back. The room was dead silent except for the sound of the two climbing the old wooden stairs. Then we heard voices. At first we couldn't understand them. I guessed that they were just on the landing at the top of the steps, when Miss Widdershins' words sounded suddenly clearly.

"He wants to trade my book for my painting? Is he insane? This is the only trade I'll give him: *a cheann mar mhalairt ar mo leabhar.* Tell him! You tell him. And it has to be tonight."

The room remained silent as Thomas trotted back down the stairs, moving loosely and easily. *A cheann mar mhalairt ar mo leabhar:* "his head for my book." Cornelia told me what it meant before I left. They had all seen a great deal of action already that day, but this was something more serious. This was one of their own.

Thomas had just reached the front door, when we heard Miss Widdershins' voice calling rapidly, "Wait, wait, wait."

She ran quickly after him, caught him and put her arms around his neck. They made their farewells on the porch. At length she let him go, and I heard the screen door slap shut. We all watched him walk away. Balin went with him.

4.

"Well, that's it then," said Cornelia. "I knew it would come to this."

We had moved to the porch.

"What will he do? I mean what will Con Gone-Away do?"

"Who knows what a traitor will do?" said Cornelia in reply. "Let's hope for the best. Goodbye, James," and she put one hand on my cheek and gave me a quick kiss on the other. It was the first time she had done this, but it didn't seem odd. Then she turned back into the house and I turned for home.

I walked with my head down, slowly, reviewing the day's events. A couple of times, when I came to a crossing, I simply stopped, lost in my thoughts, unable to make the decision to go forward. It looked like the worst was over, except for Con Gone Away and maybe for Thomas as well. I thought that one of them might not live to see the morning.

"Hey, kid!"

I looked up to see a strange man standing too close to me. He had a hand in a jacket pocket and pulled it out far enough for me to see a black handgun.

"Get in the car."

A few feet away, a car was waiting by the curb with an open door and a running engine, a long low vintage muscle car. I looked quickly around me at the empty street. I was only a block from my house, where waited warmth, safety, food, and my grandfather. It seemed impossible.

Of course, I knew not to get in a car with anyone under such circumstances. Everyone knows that. Better to take your chances and be shot on the sidewalk. But the fact is I hesitated. You might say I froze for a second, and that was long enough for the man to push me towards and halfway into the gaping opening. At that point he pulled the gun out and pointed it at me, and as I instinctively shrank away I found myself sitting in the back seat with the stranger by my side. It was not a quick-thinking performance on my part.

The driver turned around and grinned at me, and I saw the spider web tattoo on his neck.

"Hey, kid. Remember me?"

16. The Executive Branch

1.

"*You* know this kid?"

"Yeah, he's the kid from the alley. I should have known they had something to do with those freaks. Hey, kid, what do you say we go and pick up your girlfriend?"

"Good idea," I said. I would have loved to bring them to Miss Widdershins' front door. The Dragons would have cut them up for bait.

We were driving past my house. I couldn't help but look.

"Say good-bye, buddy," said the man with the spider tattoo.

We were driving south toward Northern Boulevard. I had no idea where we were headed after that.

"Frisk this guy. He might be carrying."

"What are you talking about?"

"His girlfriend had a knife. Check him out."

"He doesn't have anything. Look at him."

"Check him out. I don't want to get stabbed again."

The next few moments were embarrassing. The man made a half-hearted attempt to frisk me. He obviously had no idea what he was doing, and gave up as soon as was decently possible.

"He's clean."

When we hit Northern, the car turned right, and the men began to argue.

"What are you doing? Go left, take the Cross Island."

"I know what I'm doing."

"Take the Cross Island to the Belt."

"I know what I'm doing."

The other threw his hands up in exasperation. It came to me then that these men were clowns. That did not make them any the less dangerous, however. Quite the contrary.

We were going west, toward the city, which made me think that they were taking me to the Art Dealer. Did that mean that Walsh was wrong, and the Dealer was still in the game? As we fought our way through traffic, I looked out the window at the free people going about their business on the sidewalks. It didn't seem fair that if it weren't for the mere unfortunate fact of my sitting in this car, I would be as carefree and as safe as any of them.

Northern Boulevard seemed an odd choice of route, crowded as it was. Once as we waited idling for a light, I even noticed a parked and occupied police car in the corner lot of a fast food restaurant. I might have banged on the window and gotten their attention; I didn't believe for a moment that my captors would shoot me if I did. I decided against it, though. I knew it was bad policy to bring in the police.

"I'm gonna call him," said the driver, and began dialing a cell phone.

"Hello? Yeah. Yeah it's Hector. Yeah we picked up the kid. We're bringing him in. What?"

I could hear shouting on the other end.

"It's what you told us to do."

"What's his problem?" asked the other.

I strained to hear the words coming through the phone.

"This guy!" said Hector to his companion, shaking his head. Then, to the phone: "What's the problem? Are you afraid of Psycho? We can pick up the book, if you want to keep him quiet. It's in his trunk, I know it. I can get it right now, no problem."

More indistinct shouting.

"Man!" Hector backed off the phone for a moment. "OK. OK. I said OK. Look we're still getting paid, right? 'Cause we stuck our necks out. We still get paid. OK."

He hung up.

"What the hell?" asked the other man.

"We have to dump this kid."

"I don't think that's what he meant," I said.

"What, you mean like in the reeds or something? You know…"

He made gestures.

"I'm pretty sure that's not what he meant," I said.

I was relieved to hear the driver say: "No just leave him off."

"What the hell?"

"Somebody got to Chuckles. He's scared."

They let me off by the side of the road, and I watched them as they disappeared up an entrance ramp to the Grand Central Parkway. I was standing under some scaffolding, at the base of enormous old theater, whose entrances and windows were all filled and blocked and blinded by remorseless grey cinderblocks.

2.

I was at Flushing Main Street. I dodged across the broad divided boulevard. I knew there was a Long Island Railroad stop somewhere on Main Street, and I had only to walk up this long hill until I found it.

I was in Chinatown, a new Chinatown that had sprung up in the last couple of decades. I was amazed at the thoroughness of the metamorphosis. It was a little world in itself, with unfamiliar scripts, unfamiliar businesses, unfamiliar merchandise. I passed a grocery store, Royal Ginseng or something, with open plastic bins of shredded herbs and mushrooms laid across a stepped frame out on the sidewalk, displayed wild, so to speak, completely unlike the neat little printed packets and zip-packaged bags you'd find in a health food store. It was easy to believe the secret of health and vitality lay in those bins. The Chinese knew how to do it, I thought. Everything was out in the open, yet completely inaccessible to me. I admired them. When my father was my age, Flushing Main Street was mostly Hispanic, he said. Before that, I don't know. One of the few constants must have been the Armed Forces Recruitment Center that stood across the street, right in the middle of the action, a proud and enduring outpost of the nation, open for business. They served everyone, race, creed or color, come one, come all.

It was a longer climb to the station than I expected. I walked fast, because I was carrying something important with me. I reached the tracks, and passed beneath them, flanked on the one side by street vendors selling hundreds of DVDs arranged on shelves, some looking home-made and labeled only with magic marker, and on the other side by short order cooks slinging dumplings and the like at half a dozen windows. It was a long narrow climb up the stairs to the tracks. Apparently the king's writ didn't run here when it came to handicapped access.

As I climbed I mulled. "It's in his trunk," had said Spider Web. He was a bit of a clown, but if he was right, and Con Gone-Away was carrying the Black Book of Leuven around in his car trunk, that was a piece of news that the Dragons should receive, if I could figure out the best way to get it to them.

I waited on the platform and watched the lights spring to life as the summer night stole upon the hills and dales of Flushing. To me it was a wonderland. There was a wide empty lot beneath me, a perfect waste of urban real estate, and past that a row of little stores beneath a long line of calligraphic Chinese scrawl. On the other side of the tracks were a set of courts, demarcated by tall chain link fences, for basketball and handball and for gathering in little knots and talking. All around me there were hints of secret paths and secret lives, the beginnings of alleys that disappeared up hills and around corners, the track-level blind concrete yards loaded with junk beneath towering apartment walls.

I don't know how long I waited before I saw the lights approaching from the west and heard the rails hum. When the doors opened the platform was thronged with commuters from Manhattan coming back to their homes from work in the city, a return from the general to the particular. I found an empty seat near the door. I wanted to tell the Dragons what I had heard about Con Gone-Away and the book, but I didn't know the best way to go about it. I could get out at my stop and walk to Miss Widdershins' house, but then they would have to get in touch with Thomas and Balin. Judging from Miss Widdershins' long wait throughout the day for news to be delivered in person, I was not at all sure that any of her other agents had cell phones at the moment. My alternative was to take the train one stop farther and to get out at Gone-Away's station, and see if I could connect with the Dragons there, near his house.

I see now, and, truthfully, I probably saw then, that the prudent course of action would be to deliver the news to Miss Widdershins, and let her figure out what to do with it. Yet when the doors opened at my stop and the lines of people shuffled out, I was not among them. I sat frozen, knowing that I should move. I suppose I was tired of being a bystander, and wanted to take an active part, at my own will and no other's.

I pressed my forehead to the glass. We passed the saltwater flatlands illuminated by the glow of a rising moon just past full. When the doors opened again, I stepped out on Gone-Away's platform for the second time in my life. I followed the path up from the train, walking past a tall stately Tuscan restaurant that looked like an inn out of Old Europe, picking my way through the lot and the street where the incoming parking valets and departing commuters achieved an uneasy *modus vivendi*.

As I climbed, the streets grew quieter. By the time I turned off the main road and toward the crossroad where Cornelia and I had lost Gone-Away, I was the only one walking. I stepped lightly, cautiously; I checked the deeper shadows underneath the darkness as I approached. A thousand reconsiderations crossed my mind. This was stupid, I thought. They were probably all long gone.

A parked car flashed its headlights at me once. It was facing me, just past the crossroad. I froze. I wasn't keen to take any more forced car trips with strangers. I walked forward slowly, with my weight well back, ready to run. When I crossed the street, the lights flicked on briefly in the cab, and I recognized Balin behind the wheel. I stepped forward boldly then, and the door was opened for me.

"You again!" said Balin. "Get in."

3.

"*You* do keep turning up. What gives?"

I told the tale. It sounded ridiculous as I told it, but Balin wasn't laughing.

"In his car trunk?"

"That's what the guy, Hector, said. I don't know how accurate it is."

"That sounds like something that son of a bitch would do, drive around in the July heat with the Black Book in his trunk. He's getting ready to move now, whatever the answer he gets from the Queen, so he'd want to have it on hand."

He sat silent for a while, thinking.

"He's going to meet with Tom, in a park a little bit north of here. They're supposed to meet alone, but I'm tailing along. We assume Con Cróga will bring backup as well, if he's got anyone left. Tom's already waiting. It might get lively. Con isn't going to like what Tom has to tell him. It can't be any great surprise, though."

He looked at me.

"If we play our cards right, we just might get the book while they're talking. I might need your help. Are you game?"

"Yes. What do you want me to do?"

"I don't know yet. We'll just have to see how the hand plays out."

"What do we do now?"

"Right now, we wait."

I have heard that those words, "we wait," constitute the second most commonly uttered piece of dialogue in film. The most common is "let's go." There really isn't any other way to say either one.

Balin waited in perfect silence and perfect calm. He was long accustomed to long waiting. He did not speak, or smoke, or fidget. He showed no strain. I waited with him. I thought about my grandfather. It was getting late. He would be worried.

"Here they come," said Balin.

I looked, and I saw three men already getting into a sporty-looking vehicle a short distance up the block. I recognized Con easily, in a long coat despite the season, walking with that peculiar muscle-bound rocking motion. He sat in the front, in the driver's seat. There were two other men, both taller than he, one black, one white. One rode shotgun, one sat in the back.

"That's his car," said Balin. "Good."

He slid down in his seat and I did the same. In the shadows as we were, we would not have easily been seen. I heard the car pass and turn ahead of us.

Balin turned the key, straightened, and after a quick interval, pulled away from the curb. We saw the other car's red lights turn right. Balin didn't seem to worry about keeping them in sight. We picked them up again when we turned at the corner, going north on the only even moderately busy street on the cape. We crossed a short bridge over the railroad tracks, passed a white and brick church and a school, and made another right. Now we were on quiet side streets, surrounded by really impressive houses. There is still a lot of good comfortable money on Long Island.

We kept driving. We were on the eastern edge of the cape. Balin let the others get farther ahead and we drove without headlights. They stopped when the houses on the right side of the road gave way to parkland. They were parked by a dense stand of woods. We stopped as well, pulling up alongside a big multipart house, a compound really, just short of a marshy area that lay between us and the woods. The three men got out of the car ahead of us.

"Thomas is meeting him on the other side of that wood," said Balin. "There's a park with swings and benches and the rest of it. I want to see what these two are doing."

The three men stood for a while talking, then Con walked on alone.

"Good," said Balin. "I'm going to go for the book." Apparently he didn't consider the two remaining men to be an insurmountable obstacle. "I want you to get through that wood and keep an eye on Tommy, in case there's anyone else wandering around."

He leaned forward and punched the glove compartment open in front of me. He reached in and pulled out a handgun.

"You ever use one of these?"

He handed it to me. It was heavy for its size, and it felt clean and oiled and efficient.

"No," I said.

"Just aim down the front sight and trust in God. Give it to me for a second."

He took the gun and racked the slide.

"Now all you do is pull the trigger. Wait," he clicked a lever along the side. "The safety is now on." He pointed it out. "If you want to use it, you need to switch the safety off."

He handed the gun back to me.

"Is the safety on or off?" he asked.

"On."

"You probably won't need it. This is a precaution. Don't touch the trigger unless you're planning to shoot it. Remember, finger off the trigger. And whatever you do, don't shoot Tommy. Cornelia would never forgive you."

He looked at me, gauging my reactions, judging me by clues I didn't know I was giving.

"Worst comes to worst, just make some noise with it. Tommy will handle the rest. Forget about it unless it looks like Con brought someone else to the parley. This is really between Thomas and Con Cróga; they have business together."

He gave me a few seconds to absorb this.

"OK, let's go," he said at length. "Move quiet without being seen. There are paths through those woods if you can find them."

I opened the door softly and got out.

"One last thing," he said, and I paused, crouching by the car with the door open.

"Where do you look?"

I looked at him blankly.

"When you shoot, where do you look?"

"Down the front sights."

"Good man. Wish me luck." He grinned, and so did I.

I swung the door to shut it, but I did not hear it close. He must have caught it and eased it shut. I couldn't imagine how he intended to steal up on Gone-Away's car with those two men watching, but I had my own problems.

4.

I moved into the darkness with my gun on my hip, or as near as I could manage. I didn't trust my waistband to hold it, so after some deliberation I slipped it into a side pocket. It was a small gun. As near as I can reconstruct it in my mind, it was probably a foreign number, like an HK USP or something equivalent.

I did not crawl, dash or scurry across the ground, but moved at an even, quiet saunter. I walked across the lawn of the compound and then descended into the bordering marsh. It was a drop almost to water level and it took me out of any possible sight of the other men.

I was walking on a springy mattress of hollow reeds, most of which were lying flat, as if they had been pressed down by a light-weight steamroller. To the right I could see scattered lights gleaming on dark water. The park overlooked a very narrow neck of the sound. Walking on the reeds was familiar to me from my many excursions near my own bay. I bounced easily across and was soon scaling a dirt rise up to the solid wooded ground. I worked along the slope until I found a path leading into the woods.

The moonlight penetrated the dense growth only faintly. I stood and waited for my eyes to adjust to the deeper darkness. When I looked up, the leaves at the treetops seemed to shine in the distant light. I listened hard and walked very slowly. It was easy to get lost; there were side paths to consider. Once I was struck motionless by sudden fear, as I saw what looked like a twisted sinister troll-like figure crouched on the path directly in front of me. As I picked out the outlines, I was relieved to see that it was only a large boulder, set up to mark a place where two paths crossed. I came across a few such boulders. The paths were well-maintained and it was easy to walk quietly. I learned later that the whole area had the name and dignity of a "nature preserve."

I found myself standing on a rocky promontory, looking out

over the water. The inlet reached into a grassy flatland, much like the bay near my home, but narrower. The moon shone across the tall pale reeds and on the slick black mud that bordered the water. To the right, brackish water flowed out from the marsh, through a narrow channel in the mud, until it spread into the waters of the Sound. Closer at hand, there was a long private dock dipping its feet in the dark waters. There were no boats moored where I was, and no people to be seen. Across the water, the houses were well lit, but it seemed everyone had turned his attention inward.

I pulled myself away from this and retraced my steps, trying to find a path that led in the right direction. I was surprised suddenly by a gap in the trees, through which I could see a wide trimmed lawn, and some benches near the shore. The path I was following, which had turned west back toward the road, ran just above the park. I crouched low and kept moving. Then I heard voices, just beneath me it seemed. I stopped and leaned on a convenient boulder. I eased higher with my hands on the bare rock until I saw them through the leaves, Thomas the Rhymer and Con Cróga. They were standing out in the open, right beneath my woods, among some widely spaced trees that stood beside a gravel drive, and I could hear their words.

17. The Field

I don't think they had been speaking for very long. Con Gone-Away must have made as slow and as careful an approach as I had.

"You had better give it up, Con," said Thomas. "There's no longer any hope in it."

"Do you think so? I don't. I have the book. If you don't want it, I'll be on my way."

Thomas said something in their language.

"Yes?" Con replied. "Just you? But you still don't get the book."

"We'd take the chance of finding it. Unless you gave it to one of those idiots you work with."

Con gave a grunt of disgust.

"Hard to find good help," he said.

"Where did you come up with that lot?"

"Kusher recruited them. He's 'in the business.' All I asked him to do was nothing, and that was too much for him."

Thomas said something else. Con gave a sardonic laugh, and there followed a brief silence. I understood then that these two must have been friends once, and perhaps still were.

"So what was the Pendragon's judgement? What were her exact words?"

Thomas repeated them.

"That simple, eh? That's the Lady, still trying to hold things together with her charm and your arm. Don't you get tired of it?"

"No."

"Thomas, it's finished for them, can't you see? The Geese won't last a generation, if they're not gone already, the Cats can't even remember why they care, and the Dragons will hold together

188

only as long as she can keep throwing magic dust over them all."

"It's lasted this long."

"The Bellyboys track everything. They watch everything, they record everything. In a few years they'll be tattooing barcodes on everyone."

"That's not much of a recruitment speech."

"I'm telling you the way it is. There are no alternatives. The future holds only one way."

Thomas said something else.

"Dead men speaking a dead language," said Con. "A dead language that was alive for only a few hundred years. Died in its infancy, so sad. No one left to mourn."

"We're wasting time."

"I am trying to explain to you. She's leading you down a dead end and into a brick wall. She won't adapt. She can't adapt. She'll drag you all down with her."

"You worry too much."

"Still the loyal soldier. Still doing what Vivien says. I hope she treats you well for it."

"You talk too much. I suppose that's the way of the future, too. At present, however, one thing only matters. You stole our book. We want it back. I'm here to get it. And to settle with you if necessary. Is it necessary?"

"It is."

"Listen, Con," said Thomas with sudden vehemence. "You think you're being far sighted, but you're not. You can't last out here, not you. You'll run mad, if you haven't already. Come back, I can smooth things over."

Con laughed.

"No chance. I never look back, you know that. No, I expect quite a pleasant life. For money, you can have anything anywhere. I expect to move out to the Pacific rim. Maybe keep a harem. All shapes and sizes."

"Somewhere East of Suez, where the best is like the worst."

"Exactly."

"It will never work. They're consumers pure and simple. Everything with them is for consumption. Women, children, music, art, nature … even their religions are just something they use up and evacuate. Even their own thoughts and feelings, they're matters of interest, they use them up and empty them out. It's all just things to them. They consume everything and understand nothing. They respect nothing. You're not one of them, whatever you tell yourself."

"We'll see."

"You're not a consumer. You may be a traitor and a destroyer, but you're not a consumer. You may be an enemy, but you are still one of us."

"You worry too much."

"That's your answer."

"That's my answer."

There was a pause that seemed long, then Con spoke again.

"We'd better get this started," he said. "Does the ground suit you?"

"All ground suits me."

"I've always wondered. Haven't you?"

"Never."

"Braggart."

They were stepping away now, off the gravel track, out into the park. I moved deeper into the bushes and closer to the edge trying to keep them in view.

"Don't look so glum," said Con Gone-Away. "It's what we were born for."

2.

When I got them in view again, they were still moving away across the field, sidestepping lightly, at a good distance from one another. Off to my left were a set of swings and a slide and a tee-ter-totter and some of the other paraphernalia of play; they kept well clear of all that and moved over open grass. Con Gone-Away already had a sword in his hand, and I saw Thomas reach under his coat and pull out his own blade. He must have had a scabbard rigged, maybe under his arm and behind his back. It was not a long rapier this time, as it had been in Miss Widdershins' yard, but a shorter sword with a hand guard, like an old Scottish basket hilt or what they used to call a back sword, with a single sharp edge. Con's sword might have been its twin, the weapon of choice in their set. Both held them in a high guard, tip directed towards the other.

At a certain point – I saw no signal – they found the ground they wanted, and settled down to it. I could see it was work they knew. There can have been few duels like it on the continent, certainly not in the last two hundred years. Maybe not ever. I can recall few specifics of the fight, and not because of the time elapsed. I tried to write it all down within the week, but it was over my head. The esoterica of swordsmanship, and of that type of swordsmanship in particular, where the goal is blood not applause, were and are beyond me. I could see that there was no movement without purpose, but I could not see what the purposes might be.

There was no constant clash of edges such as I had grown to expect from screen and stage. Most of the duel occurred at a great distance, where neither could have touched the other even after a long lunge, and the action was a constant calibration of distance and angle, of stealing advantage as only they could see it. More than once, when they teetered at the edge of a clash, one would suddenly break off, back away, and then they would start working their way towards each other again.

Con Gone-Away was fast, active, crouching low and bouncing across the ground on tireless legs like pistons. Well out of distance he would sometimes rock back and forth and flex each leg to keep loose, so that he looked almost to be dancing. Thomas stood taller and moved slower and quieter. He looked to be more of a technician than Con Gone-Away, but I can't say that with any certainty. The reluctance with which he started the fight seemed to have melted away, as the duel imposed its own inexorable logic on them both. All thought and memory of books and paintings, of Dragons and Bellymen, faded from our minds as the whole world was reduced to the arena.

I can remember three passes, though there may have been more. There probably were. At some point they must have doffed their coats but I have no recollection of them doing so. On all occasions when they closed together, I had the impression that the opportunity was created and decision was made before the play of weapons, when they were still at a distance, and the actual meeting of steel was just the completion of a much longer move.

On the first pass, it was Con who made the attack, seizing some chance created by a hitch in the paired movements, rocketing in and catching Thomas in the act of a hurried retreat. I couldn't see if his thrust found a home, though I thought he might have touched Thomas' sword arm on the forearm, which would have been a dangerous wound indeed. I could, however, see Con slip in the grass, as his front foot went out from under him at the end of his lunge. Thomas had been moving back, but he came in fast. Con stayed on all fours and scampered rapidly sideways across the ground like a crab, until he could bounce up at last with his point at the ready. Whatever the rules, and it is plain there were such, apparently a man was responsible for his own footing.

After this clash, Thomas became more aggressive, pressing the action, stepping forward, although always with caution. The intensity of the duel seemed to transport us all outside the current of time, the combatants and the spectator, and the field of battle as well. On the second pass, Con was again the aggressor, but this time he came in with a short step and a feint and I heard the expected clash of bade on blade, and he followed it with a longer attack, another thrust. Thomas was fighting at the time with his free arm in a guard position, with his left hand about even with his right elbow, and it looked to me that he took a long slice on the outside of that arm. Con let his momentum carry him past this time, and as Thomas pivoted to keep him in view he aimed a high backhand cut at his passing opponent. When they faced each other again, having exchanged places, I saw Thomas wringing his left arm in a peculiar way, as though to test it, and Con bleeding from a cut under his left eye.

Oddly enough, these near misses only made them both more

violent rather than less. Maybe Con became too impatient. On the third pass it was Thomas who attacked and this time when they met, all motion ceased for a split second as they hung together. Then I saw Thomas pull back his elbow, drawing his sword back out. His thrust had hit solid. As Con sank to the earth, Thomas stepped back a short pace and finished with a quick vicious cut at his neck. It was over.

For a moment, Thomas stood over his former enemy, then he fell to his knees alongside his body. I thought at first that he had been wounded too and I am not to this day sure that he wasn't. Then I heard a voice, and it was Thomas, and he seemed to be declaiming. I started hearing sounds again, the sounds of the world, and among them I heard a siren wailing. I looked about me and remembered that this was not some lost arena out of time, but a municipal park, bounded by a street full of houses, and overlooked, even if at some distance, by dozens of windows.

I heard a horn honking and, pushing my way deeper into the bushes, I looked left and saw the road, and Balin standing alongside his car, reaching in and leaning on the horn.

"Thomas!" he called. "Let's go. That siren is for us."

Thomas remained where he was.

Balin honked one more time.

"Let's go, Tommy. I got the book. Leave him."

There are times for waiting, and this wasn't one of them. Balin jumped back in the car and drove into the park along the gravel path. He stopped some distance from the body; maybe the ground was soft and he didn't want to run the risk of getting stuck. He opened the door, ran over and lifted the mourner to his feet. Thomas woke out of his trance and made for the car, while Balin stooped to retrieve Gone-Away's sword. When they were both in the car, Balin backed away, did a quick turn and headed for the paved road. Not a moment too soon. Balin's car disappeared behind the houses beyond the edge of the park, and almost simultaneously I heard a police car approaching from the other end of that road. I backed out of the bushes onto the trail through the woods.

3.

I moved back along the path, fast. I wanted distance, as much and as quick as I could get it. When I got to the edge of the wooded plateau, I crashed through the last bushes and slid down to the mattress of reeds. I was sure that there would be more police cars coming along the road, and I made the split second decision to keep by the water. I bounded across the reeds and found myself crouched at the foot of another dirt rise. On this side, the plateau above me was populated by houses not by trees, but I thought if I stayed low, at the level of water and weed, I could escape notice. If I were seen and detected, I couldn't imagine what excuse I could give for being there, fleeing the scene of a killing. Already I was regretting my decision to take refuge in the salt marsh.

I had to pass the long dock, which jutted out from the compound next to which Balin and I had parked. I passed beneath, stepping over and ducking under the slippery wood posts, with my feet sucking through mud. There seemed to be no one at home in the compound. It may have been a day care center or day school of some kind; there were plastic playground structures on the back lawn.

As I moved along the shore, I came to realize that the neck I was navigating was getting narrower and narrower, and soon I would be in back yards. If I kept going I would be back on the very street I was trying to avoid. Looking east I saw across a channel of water welcoming trees, and wider expanses of marshes, and above them quiet streets untroubled by the alarum behind me. I had only to cross the dark channel and not to be seen doing it.

I slid down the black mud and into the water. I had hardly gotten my feet wet when they slipped in two different directions and I found myself sitting in shallow water. I started forward again, first on all fours, then standing as the water got deeper. I kept a wide stance and tried to crouch low to diminish my profile. When I was hip deep, I was struck by a sudden notion. I forced my hand into my wet jeans pocket and retrieved the gun, which I let sink into water and the mud. At least now, if I were picked up, I would not have to explain what I was doing with a concealed weapon.

That was as deep as the water got. Soon I was in the shallows again, taking one more fall for good measure just when I had almost reached dry land, startling some ducks up into the air. I grabbed two handfuls of the tough cordgrass and pulled myself back to my feet. I struggled across the trackless marsh toward a stand of trees that stood on the edge of dry land. When I climbed up among them I was in a little park again, a sort of younger cousin of the nature preserve on the other side, with an easy dirt path to the street and even a plaque at the entrance.

This turned out to be the worst part of the day, the closest to a nightmare. I was tired, wet, and thirsty, but I was back on the paved sidewalks, and I had only to walk away from the water, so I thought, to reach the boulevard and the way home. Instead I seemed to be trapped in a labyrinth, closed off on every side, by the waters of the sound to the north and by the high ridge of the railroad tracks to the south. Everywhere I turned, it seemed, there was a dead end sign, or a high chain link fence, or the sudden appearance of water. I could have climbed the fence and gone over the tracks, but I didn't want to be seen doing so, and I couldn't believe it was necessary. It all seemed unreasonable, impossible. The people who lived here had to get in and out just like everyone else.

When I passed the same little block of attached duplexes for the third time and found myself back at the park, I had a sudden deranged fear that I would never get out, and that perhaps day would never come, but I'd wander these streets forever. It passed, however, like everything else. I simply took the alternate route away from the park, a route that I had overlooked for some reason, and I was soon walking along a straight wide well-lit avenue and approaching the lowered arms and flashing lights of a railroad crossing. I look at a map now and I see a few short streets and can't imagine how I got so confused.

At the crossing, I waited for the train to pull away, too tired to look for a path around or under it. I felt conspicuous with the caked black mud on the seat of my pants and my knees, and on my pant legs where I had wiped my hands. I was conscious of the smell of the bay on me, that complex and unpleasant smell of salt water and many dead things, both animal and vegetable, reeds and grasses, clams, fish and crabs. Of the few people in and around the station, though, none had any attention to spare for me. I was young enough that my disheveled state was not all that remarkable.

After the gates opened and I continued pressing along towards the boulevard, I became aware of a helicopter in the distance, hovering over the little cape I had so lately left, searching, so I surmised, for the two fugitives. It was joined by another that swooped in, passing directly above me, lit up like a Christmas tree, and together they performed a patterned search that swiftly widened its field. They looked rather like a pair of dragons themselves.

Just as I reached the boulevard, two police cars with sirens screaming passed before my face, headed west. Although I did not think anyone was looking for me, I felt a strong necessity to avoid that one road, the first crossing south of the water, the main artery, along which the police would no doubt be hurrying for the rest of the night. Instead, I took a long loop south, which took me up a slope lined by the night-lit houses of oblivious Bellymen, then along the service road of the Long Island Expressway, and then, where the Expressway crossed a perpendicular Parkway, along a footpath that branched off and led past a whirling tangle of entrances and exits, touching all but beholden to none, until it deposited me back in the city streets.

I was tired; my detour was adding five miles to the walk home. I sat down to rest once, on a stump, in a nice little niche surrounded by trees. I sat and I listened to the night. There were still faint sounds of the chase in the distance. I took that to be a good sign, especially since they seemed to be diffused over a wide area. I was tempted to go to sleep, but when I arose, I found myself much refreshed. The walking went easier; I established a nice rhythm. The mud had begun drying on my pants, showing a much lighter, less conspicuous color. By the time I reached home, it was beginning to flake off in places.

Lights were on in the house, and when I opened the door I found my grandfather asleep in the recliner in front of the television, in front of a show he never would have watched. I turned it off, then went to the bathroom where I washed my hands and threw water in my face for a long time. When I got out, my grandfather was waiting for me.

"You're back. How long have you been home?"

"Just a few minutes."

"I fell asleep. What time is it?"

When I looked at the clock and told him, he said: "So late? Why are you home so late? I was worried about you."

"We had a lot to do," I said.

"I was worried. Your parents are worried. When they called you hadn't come home yet. I suppose it's too late to call them now. But first thing in the morning we should."

He looked at me keenly.

"You don't usually stay out so late. Are you sure you're OK?"

I don't think he even noticed the mud.

"I'm OK," I said.

"And there's nothing wrong?"

"No," I said. "Everything is fine."

18. The End

1.

The killing made a splash in the local news, though not quite as big a splash as I expected. I listened to the radio, watched hours of television, and bought three local newspapers. Against the odds, both Balin and Thomas had escaped. As I pieced the story together, it appeared that the good offices of witnesses may have inadvertently aided my escape as well.

When the police first arrived at the park, I read, they were responding to the report of a disturbance. Probably they had expected a drunken brawl among teenagers, or maybe a shouting match with the householders. They had arrived, without special urgency, in a single car, which allowed the Dragons to get a good start and to pass over one of the only two roads out of the cape before both were sealed. The casual approach lasted only until the police discovered the freshly slain body in the park. At that point, one or more helpful witnesses emerged from the bordering houses and described what they had seen. They described a fight, three men, and a getaway car, but of course had nothing to say about anyone else. The chase had focused entirely on the car, and no one had ever been looking for me.

I never heard anything about the two guards Con had taken with him, the two men who stayed with his car. I was relieved about that; it meant that Balin hadn't done anything permanent with them, but had somehow persuaded them both to leave. Information about the victim was sparse. When he was described in the news, it was under an alias, first one, then another. No one could find out much about him, what he did or where he came from, but the discovery of a number of improbable *objets d'art* among his effects gave color to the suspicion that he was involved in shady dealings of some kind. I imagine our Art Thief was quaking when he read that, but I never heard that he was brought into the investigation. No doubt he took a few items off display and buried them in the back room.

The hue and cry faded quickly, probably because there was so little information readily available, and the media moved on to easier stories. By the time my parents and sister returned, two days after the combat, it was almost possible to miss the story entirely. My grandfather took some mild interest in the unusual occurrence, but he never connected it to my late night out.

It was a week before anyone in my family noticed that they hadn't seen Cornelia for some time, and that I hadn't been over to the big house. My mother was the first to ask me about it.

"I think they're away," I said, which was true enough.

Two weeks passed before I took the walk over to Miss Widdershins' house, already afraid of what I'd find. When I walked up the path, I looked with apprehension at the lengthening grass on either side of me. I knocked on the screen door, and no one rose to greet me. I knocked for a while, then walked to the rear of the house and knocked on that door too, expecting nothing and getting it. Finally I sat down on the side steps. They were gone, and I did not expect them back. Their time had come, and they had moved on.

I don't know how long I had been sitting there, when I heard a plaintive mew. The little grey kitten, four months older than when I first saw it, had climbed the stairs and was winding itself around my legs. I stroked its fur, and it arched its back in appreciation, but I had nothing else to give it. When I finally walked away, it followed me for quite a distance, calling plaintively. It too would have to learn to do without the Widdershins household.

Time passed, and my mother at last asked point blank.

"I haven't seen Cornelia for a while," she said casually when all four of us were gathered. "Are they still away on a trip?"

"They're gone," I answered. "I don't think they're coming back."

"They left just like that? Did they say goodbye?"

"No."

"That's terrible," said my sister indignantly. "I think that's really mean. I wouldn't have expected that of them."

"It's OK," I said. "I always knew they'd have to leave some time. I am not surprised."

"Did they leave a forwarding address?" asked my father.

"No."

"But did they sell the house?"

"I don't know," I said, though I was fairly sure that they did not. It seemed to me that their wealth was in real estate, in old real estate, and they would only give that up with the greatest reluctance.

"That's awful," said my mother. "You got along so well."

I was anxious that my family not think poorly of the Dragons.

"It's all right," I said. "I'm sure I'll see them again."

They were especially nice to me for a long time after that, and walked softly about me as if I were a convalescent.

I have not told them about the Dragons, and the other tribes, and about our connection to them. In the first place, I couldn't find the words, and in the second place, I don't know how much it would matter. We already knew as a family that we were different from everyone else, my mother and grandfather as well, although they had no connection to the tribes save by marriage. In any case, I haven't gotten around to it yet. Maybe some day I will show them this account.

2.

I tried the house two more times before the summer ended, just to be sure. The first time, the grass was long and I could see at a glance that no one was living within. There were weeds in the flower beds and a couple of blown branches, from a recent storm, lay in the driveway. They were only subtle touches, to be sure, but it was plain to me that the guiding hand had been removed, and the place, left to its own devices, was reverting to a natural state. I saw the kitten again on the way home, but this time it ignored me.

It was already learning to do for itself.

The second time, I had a sudden wild hope as I approached, for the pale green lawn had been freshly mowed. I paid for that brief happiness, though, when the moment's hope proved to be a false one. The flowers were now quite overgrown by thickening weeds and no one answered when I knocked. They must have sent someone around to tidy the place up a bit. I remembered the other Dragon house, the one connected through the garages. I thought about walking around to the back and knocking there, but I didn't really want to do it. In the absence of Miss Widdershins and Cornelia, I didn't know what I would say to the others, or what I would ask them. If they want to send word, I thought, they will do so. This time there was no cat. I liked to think that whoever mowed the lawn had picked it up and carried it back to Cornelia.

Going back to school was difficult, but not quite as difficult as I had feared. In the past I had always been careful to preserve an ironical distance from the school world, from both the ruling officialdom and the modified prison society beneath it. I found now that no such effort was necessary. I was like an exchange student who was over for one semester and only understood enough of the language to ask for the salt at table and to smile and to nod. It was perhaps even more boring than it had been in the past, but now unthreatening. There was plenty of work to be done, sophomore year being harder by a degree than freshman, but I was always able enough for that.

I retained the companionship of my small circle of friends, Trey still chief among them, now that his obsession had shrunk to claim a more proportionate share of his attention. Over the summer he had discovered ju jitsu, which seemed to foster a more relaxed approach than had bodybuilding. Trey still lifted weights, he explained, but now as a means to an end, not an end in itself. Trey studied traditional Japanese ju jitsu, in all its formality and behavioral rigor, and he distained the possibility of a vulgar conflict with brawling wrestlers. He moved gravely about the school like a black Japanese Kwai Chang Caine, if such a thing can be imagined. Heyward regarded us apparently as a source of mutual merriment, and grinned at us whenever he chanced to see us, as if we all shared a secret joke. He was busy making a name for himself at the state level as a wrestler. Tucci still didn't like me.

Troll entered the Marines, just as he planned. I get letters from him, mostly humorous, first postmarked from Parris Island, and later from his various deployments. Lacking a college diploma, he went in as a grunt. He's a lance corporal now. He seems to be content, although I wouldn't exactly say that he's enjoying himself. I've only seen him twice since he went in. We played ping pong again.

My sister is attending a small liberal arts college in northern Massachusetts, with a nationally known music program. The whole family joined forces to scrape up enough money to send her. It's a good thing my grandfather paid off our mortgage many years ago, so we can all live cheap. Even so, she will graduate with a liberal arts degree and a pile of debt. It's a colder, duller, quieter house without her.

3.

So the years have passed.

I keep checking the Internet, some particular sources I have discovered, to see if there has been any progress on the Gone-Away case. They never found the getaway car, which is a good thing, as it must have been positively patterned with fingerprints, including mine. They did find Con's car that first day, by the side of the road, but there was nothing in it. If they managed to lift the prints of Con's ersatz bodyguards from the car, and pulled the two of them in for questioning, I don't think they could have found out much from them, except Balin's description. Depending on how much they knew, I suppose they might have made some trouble for Kusher the Art Thief, but last time I checked he was still doing business at the same old stand.

I wonder sometimes about DNA: had Thomas left some on the field of battle, and if so did that spell the end of his service as champion? Was he now "in the system"? I don't know if the gun ever surfaced in the tide, but even if it did, in highly degraded state, it was never used in a crime, at least not by me.

I continued to check the houses at intervals. It wasn't long before a "For Sale" sign went up on the lawn of the other Dragon house, and it wasn't long after that the sign came down again, and the house with it. They've built another McMansion there, rather more tasteful than most. Clearly, the people who live in it now are not Dragons.

Miss Widdershins' house told a different story. It was empty a good year, but cared for regularly, with even the walk shoveled in the winter. Then one day, towards the end of the summer before my junior year, when at the end of a long walk I bent my steps toward the old lair, I was surprised to see two children playing on the front lawn, one of them struggling to get a tricycle going on the grass. They were very young, plainly brother and sister. I stood and I stared.

A man came out the screen door, drying his hands on a towel. He was a big man with a bull neck and a mustache, with a distinct fireman's air about him. He wore a dark t-shirt decorated with an insignia. He came down the steps, hanging the towel on the railing. I looked, but I couldn't tell by looking. I spoke.

"Hi," I said. "Excuse me, but I used to visit here all the time. I had a friend who lived here. I was wondering do you know the people who used to live in this house?"

The man shook his head.

"Can't say that I do," he said. "We only moved in a couple of weeks ago."

"Do you know … did they by any chance leave any kind of address where they can be reached?"

"Sorry, kid, no."

"OK, thanks."

I began walking away, and I must have looked very sad, because I had only gone a few steps before the man called to me.

"Hey, kid!"

I stopped and turned.

"Be patient," he said.

We looked at each other for a long moment, then both turned away.

He was not a Dragon, I later decided, but must have been a Goose, given the use of the house. Did that mean the sovereignty had been established to everyone's satisfaction, or was it a simple courtesy, such as one tribe would give the other as a matter of course? I never knew, but it was a happy meeting.

Not long after that, I received one last token. I was returning home from school at the beginning of junior year, the most serious year of them all, when college comes into view, and the talk is all of SATs and AP courses and extracurricular activities. I had paused before the front door, to smooth away the grumpiness before I entered, when I looked to our old drop box, perhaps to cheer myself with memories. I noticed a silver thread hanging out the front. When I lifted the flap and drew up the thread, I found it tied around a ring of gold. The ring had been neatly cut in half, with beveled edges at each end of the semicircle. The ring was tied in the middle with a silken thread; it was thick, heavy, of real gold. It was a trick out of an old song. She would like that.

So I am patient. Sometimes it seems a long waiting. I do dream of them, of course, sometimes of what was and sometimes whole new episodes, of what might have been. Most of all I remember the singing, the choruses that made time stop, the old Gallic wine of the Dragons and the swift brightness of the Geese. Best of all is when I lie between sleep and waking, either falling back into the world of dreams or slowly leaving it. It is then that I truly feel myself back at the house, with Miss Widdershins seated at the top of the steps with a glass of the fierce bright gold in her hand, and Cornelia and I seated below at some silly game, together behind an unseen and unbreakable fence of sharp steel, with never a care for the world outside, as it was once and as it will be again.

Terence Gallagher lives in Queens, New York, where he grew up and to which he keeps returning. He studied classics, with a side of bagpiping, in Massachusetts and medieval history in Toronto and spent a dozen years or so as an academic librarian, mostly in southwest Florida. He has published short stories and poetry in small journals in the US and UK. This is a first novel.